DEAD
IS JUST
A DREAM

OTHER BOOKS BY MARLENE PEREZ

DEAD IS JUST A DREAM

marlene perez

Houghton Mifflin Harcourt

Boston   New York

Harcourt is an imprint of Houghton Mifflin Harcourt Publishing Company.
www.hmhbooks.com

Text set in Adobe Jenson Pro

Library of Congress Cataloging-in-Publication Data

Perez, Marlene.
Dead is just a dream / Marlene Perez.
pages cm.—(Dead is)
Summary: Paranormal warrior Jessica Walsh enlists the help of her psychic neighbor,
Daisy Giordano, to help discover who or what is causing Nightshade, California,
residents to die in their sleep with horrified looks on their faces.
ISBN 978-0-544-10262-0 (hardback)
[1. Supernatural—Fiction. 2. Nightmares—Fiction. 3. Murder—Fiction.
4. Psychic ability—Fiction. 5. High schools—Fiction. 6. Schools—Fiction.
7. Interpersonal relations—Fiction.] I. Title.
PZ7.P4258Ddi 2013
[Fic]—dc23
2013003883

Manufactured in the United States of America
DOC 10 9 8 7 6 5 4 3 2 1
4500426851

To my darlings Uno and Dos

CHAPTER ONE

It got chilly on the beach at night. Cold sand between my toes made me shiver. I got up and threw another log on the fire.

"I can't believe summer is almost over," Eva said. She snuggled closer to her boyfriend, Evan.

"The sooner, the better," said Andy. She flipped her curly blond hair in her haughty way. "We've gotten soft during the summer."

"Flo was on her honeymoon part of the time," I pointed out. Flo was our trainer and head virago — woman warrior — which meant she was pretty much our boss.

"We still should have worked out every day," Andy said sternly. "Instead of spending all our time at the beach."

"We played volleyball and ran on the sand," Raven said. "That's still working out." Raven was petite with dark hair. She'd grown it out this summer, and it hung down her back in a long braid. She didn't look anything like her brother, Dominic, who was tall and blond. He resembled his aunt Katrina and his mom, but I knew from photos that Raven looked like her dad.

Dominic stared at the fire. "I can't believe it's my senior year."

I had to bite my lip to keep from blurting out that I didn't want to talk about it. Senior year and then what? He'd go off to college or move to LA to make it in the music business or something and we'd be over.

He glanced at my face and seemed to read some of what I was feeling, because he added, "I don't want to think about tomorrow. I just want to enjoy tonight."

He ran a hand through his hair, which had become even blonder over the summer.

"Not me," Andy said. "I can't wait for senior year to start. The sooner it starts, the sooner it's done and I can get to the good stuff."

The "good stuff" for Andy usually involved kicking someone's or something's butt. The town of Nightshade had been surprisingly quiet lately, so she was spoiling for a fight.

"School doesn't start until Monday," Raven said. "We have the whole weekend. And look at that moon!"

I craned my neck to look, and leaned back into Dominic, who put his arms around me. The crescent moon was obscured by a heavy fog.

"Jessica, do you hear that?" Andy asked.

"Hear what?"

"That thumping noise."

"Sounds like something running," Raven said.

The "something" came into view. A ghostly white horse raced along the sand, hooves thundering as it went. Its eyes glowed red as it let out an ear-splitting whinny, and I was immobilized by a sickly dread. The whirlwind tattoo on my arm that alerted me of danger didn't just tingle. It burned.

I screamed.

A second later, the horse vanished.

"That was awesome," Eva breathed. "Reminds me of the *Legend of Sleepy Hollow* — except without the Headless Horseman." My best friend was a big horror movie fan and budding filmmaker.

Dominic shivered and said, "I always wondered what paralyzing fear felt like. Now I know."

I nudged him. "I thought you never got scared."

"I do now," he said. "That was freaky." He picked up his guitar and strummed it shakily. A familiar blank look passed over his face, and then the first lyrics of "Wild Horses" came out of his mouth.

When the song ended, everyone stared at him.

"Is that a new one?" Andy asked.

Raven rolled her eyes. "It was a Rolling Stones song, from like when your grandparents were kids."

"I've never played that before in my life," Dominic said.

My boyfriend was a seer who made predictions through song. They were usually warnings or clues to mysteries we needed to solve. Something was definitely up.

Andy's dad came to check on us. "How's it going?" he asked. "Ready to head up to the house?" Andy and her dad lived in a cute place overlooking the beach.

"Al-almost," Andy said.

"You look like you've all seen a ghost," her dad said. He quickly realized he might have sounded tactless, and tried backtracking. "Sorry. I can't believe I just said that after what happened."

What had happened was that a few months ago, we'd found a dead body in the cave on the beach. The cave had been barricaded shortly thereafter.

Since then, we had to beg our parents, repeatedly, to let us have a bonfire on the beach. They'd only let us because we'd agreed to chaperones — plural. My parents were taking a walk down the beach, but my guess was they'd be back in a minute or two.

"We were telling ghost stories," I finally said. I wasn't going to mention that we'd just seen a ghostly horse. They'd lock us in our rooms and throw away the keys, even though half of our little group were viragoes.

Dominic kissed me on my forehead. "It's almost time to go anyway," he said. "How about if I give you a ride home? I want to play you my new song."

"What about me?" Raven said kiddingly.

"I thought you were spending the night here," Andy said, then realized that Raven was just messing with her brother.

"Let me check with my parents," I said to Dominic. "They've been protective lately." I couldn't really blame them. My parents were usually pretty laid back, because they had a lot of kids to keep track of. Eight, to be exact. I had one older brother and six younger sisters.

Mom and Dad walked back to the bonfire holding hands. "It's such a gorgeous night," Mom said.

They obviously hadn't seen the red-eyed demon horse or she wouldn't be saying that.

"Mrs. Walsh, is it okay if Jessica comes over to my house for an hour or two?" Dominic asked.

She gave him a long, considering look that moms always seem to have in their arsenal.

"My mom will be there," he added quickly.

"Is Lydia staying in Nightshade long?" Dad asked.

5

It was doubtful. Dominic's mom was a virago, like me, only she didn't protect just one town. Lydia Gray was a freelance virago, on call wherever she was needed most, which meant she spent a lot of time away from her family. Dominic and Raven lived with their aunt.

Dominic shrugged. "I think her plans are uncertain right now. She travels a lot for business."

"And what business is that?" Mom asked. I shot her a stop-being-nosy look, but she ignored me. My parents, along with most of Nightshade, were unaware of the existence of viragoes protecting the town from danger.

"We'd better get going," I said.

Dominic grabbed our guitars and we walked toward his car.

"So senior year, huh?"

"Yep," he said. "That's kind of what my new song is about."

"Senior year?"

"No, after senior year."

"You want me to listen to a song about you leaving me?"

He pulled me close. "We'll talk every day." My relationship with Dominic was just starting to feel like something I could count on, but I knew I couldn't. My brother, Sean, and his girlfriend, Samantha, were still together, despite doing the long-distance thing during college, but they were an exception. I wasn't sure Dominic and I would be.

"What about college?" I asked.

"I'm taking a year off," he said. "That's what I wanted to talk to you about. Side Effects May Vary is going on tour."

"You're going to be on tour for a whole year?" I couldn't keep the alarm out of my voice.

"Not the whole time," he admitted. "But I will be gone a lot." Side Effects May Vary had won the Battle of the Bands a few months ago and the grand prize was a recording contract with Cranky Kitten Records.

I waited, but Dominic didn't say anything else for a long moment.

"What do you think?" he finally said.

"Does it matter?" I snapped. "Sounds like you have it all planned out already."

"Jess, don't be like that," he said softly.

"Like what?"

"Mad."

I sighed. "I'm not mad. Just disappointed," I said. "But I'll try to make the best of it."

We made the drive to his house in silence.

Katrina, his aunt, had a little bungalow with a swing on the front porch. Dominic pulled into the driveway.

"Can you do me a favor?" he asked.

I nodded.

"Don't mention the tour to my mom," he said. "I haven't had a chance to talk to her about it yet."

"Okay," I said. "It's not like your mom and I have long chats anyway." Truth was, Lydia Gray avoided me and I wasn't sure why.

The house was dark. "It looks like we have the place to ourselves," Dominic said. He gave me a long kiss, not bothering to turn on a light.

Which is why I jumped about a foot when light flooded the room.

Dominic's mom stood there, next to a tall brunette girl with smoky blue eyes.

"Tash!" Dominic said. "What are you doing here?"

"Surprising you, of course," she replied. "Can't a girl surprise her boyfriend?"

Dominic grabbed my hand as I tried to step away from him. I resisted, but he brought me to his side anyway. "Tashya, it's *ex-girlfriend* and you know it. This is Jessica, my girlfriend. Jessica, this is Tashya Bennington. We used to go out when we were sophomores back at my old school."

"Nice to meet you," I said. I held out my hand but she ignored me. I had no doubt she saw the kiss and heard Dominic call me his girlfriend, but she was pretending to be oblivious.

She turned to Dominic's mom. "Mrs. Gray, I'm starving. Is there anywhere to eat in this town?" Her tone made it apparent she didn't think much of Nightshade, and I bristled.

"I'll fix you something," Mrs. Gray said. "You had a long drive."

They went into the kitchen without Tashya even acknowledging me.

"Nice to meet you, Tashya," I called after her, but I didn't really mean it.

Dominic drew me into a hug. "I don't know what she's doing here, but I'm sure she'll be gone by tomorrow," he assured me.

But Tashya didn't go away.

CHAPTER TWO

Saturday, Eva came over to decide what we were going to wear the first day of school. She had a duffel bag full of stuff, which she spread out on my bed.

"Mom bought me tons of sweaters," she said. "I don't know what she was thinking. The temperature is still in the eighties."

"I know," I said. "I think I'm going with a sundress."

"Evan got me a really cool Godzilla tee when he was on vacation. I'm going to wear that with a pair of shorts. At least I have some new sandals."

"Maybe I'll go with shorts and a tee too," I said. "What do you think of this shirt?" I held up a top I had borrowed from my sister Sarah.

"I think the pink one is cuter," she replied.

"With my red hair?"

"Why not?" Eva said. "You look great in pink."

"Maybe," I said. "What about this one instead?" I held

up a dark green top. "It's a little dressier than a tee, but it'll look good with these shorts."

Eva lost interest in fashion. "So what did you and Dominic do after the bonfire?" she asked. "Was it romantic?"

"It was," I admitted. "Until his ex-girlfriend showed up. But that doesn't change the fact that, sooner or later, he's leaving."

"That's not for ages. And besides, he'll be back. In the meantime, why not enjoy what you have?"

"You're right," I replied. "I'll try."

"We should go on a double date tonight," Eva said. "Does Dominic have a gig?"

"No. We were just going to rent a movie."

"Let's do something different," she said.

"Like what?" I asked.

"There's the art exhibit."

"What art exhibit?"

"Ms. Johns told me about it last time I was at the library," Eva said. "It's Jensen Kenton. There will be other art displayed too, but Jensen Kenton is the big draw."

"The landscape artist? Not even my grandparents like his stuff."

She shrugged. "It's something to do."

"I'll talk to Dom," I said.

"Good," she replied. "Now try this on."

She tossed me a T-shirt with a galloping horse on it. I frowned. "This reminds me of the ghostly horse we saw last night."

"Give it back, then." She held out her hand. "I can't wait until you find out what that's all about."

We decided to go to the art show, so Dominic picked me up and we drove to the library. The exhibit had been set up in the community room. Eva and Evan were waiting in the hallway. They were staring at something in one of the glass cases that lined the walls.

"Sorry we're late," I said. "I couldn't find my phone."

"Jessica, come check out these marionettes," Eva said. "They're amazing."

Row after row of wooden marionettes filled the cases. They were amazing all right, but kind of disturbing. Some were just puppet heads mounted on thin metal sticks. There were princesses in elaborate ball gowns, unicorns and elves, elephants and zebras, and even some clowns. In the next case, there was a troupe of skeletons, dressed in mariachi outfits.

"Wouldn't this one be perfect for a horror movie?" Eva said. She was pointing to an all-black figure, its face concealed by a mask holding the strings of an even smaller marionette. I gave it a closer look. The title was "Master Manipulator."

The exhibit was crowded, but I was relieved there was no sign of Dominic's ex-girlfriend.

"I didn't expect to see so many people here," Dominic commented.

"Me, neither," Evan said. "Just goes to show there's not much to do in Nightshade on a Saturday night."

If he only knew. It had been quiet in Nightshade all summer long, but it wasn't going to last. I could just feel it. Of course, I had an advantage that Evan didn't. My whirlwind tattoo had sounded an alarm at the beach, which meant trouble was on its way.

Most of the crowd was gathered in front of a huge landscape painting. There were gasps and muttered comments as they stared. Dominic grabbed my hand and said, "Let's see what all the fuss is about."

The nighttime scene seemed innocuous until we looked closer and discovered the hidden images.

"What's that standing in the shadows?" Dominic leaned in and pointed. Upon closer inspection, I saw werewolves whose fangs were dripping with blood.

Another painting was of a large red mouth, crammed full of glistening cockroaches.

"Gross!" I said.

The next display held four paintings. They were just as bad. On the surface the first one looked like a relaxing ocean scene with waves crashing on the shore, but underneath the waves was a huge horse nibbling on a dead whale.

"This is different from Jensen Kenton's previous work," Eva said. "Very different."

An older man in jeans and an Andy Warhol tee overheard her. "You like it? I thought the residents of Nightshade might appreciate my new direction."

Eva looked at the next piece, which was a city engulfed in flames while a demon roasted what looked like a man on a spit. "Uh, you have an unusual idea about what people like."

"It's supposed to represent the four seasons," the man explained.

"I don't get it," Evan said.

"I don't like it," Eva said. I nudged her. I had a hunch we were talking to the artist himself, which was confirmed when the guy held out his hand.

"I'm Jensen Kenton, and you're not supposed to *like* it," he said. "It's supposed to make you think."

"It'll probably give me nightmares," I said.

The comment seemed to please him. He smiled widely. "It's been a pleasure, but now I must meet my other guests."

Dominic waited until Mr. Kenton had left and then said, "Why don't we blow off the rest of the exhibit and get a burger at Slim's instead?"

"Sounds good," I said. "I should check in with Flo about what happened on the beach last night anyway." Flo, who worked as a waitress at our favorite diner, had a tattoo that matched mine. And Raven's and Andy's. Actually, Flo had several tattoos, one for every year she'd been a virago. I figured Dominic's mom had some, too, but we never talked about it.

"We should leave now or we might not have any appetite left," Eva said.

On our way out, we saw a sad-looking clown torturing balloons into animal shapes in a corner.

"Who would bring a kid to this exhibit?" Dominic asked.

"Maybe he's a performance artist," Eva suggested.

"Or maybe just the regular kind," I said. I pointed to the wall behind the clown. It was covered with sad-eyed clown paintings.

"Ugh. Clowns," Eva said.

I agreed with her. Clowns gave me the creeps.

The disturbing paintings stayed with me even after we'd left the exhibit.

The diner was busy, and we grabbed the last open table. Slim's was the most popular place in town. It was decorated with lots of stainless steel and red leather. Flo's brother, Griffin, owned the place, but everyone called him Slim because of his semitransparent nature.

Connor Archer came over to take our order. "I didn't know you worked here," I said. Connor was a year ahead of me in school.

"Hi, Jessica, everybody," he said. "I just started, so go easy on me."

Dominic grabbed my hand under the table. I gave it a reassuring squeeze. He didn't have anything to worry about. Connor used to have a bit of a crush on me, but had been dating Selena Silvertongue for the past few months.

"Flo would kill us if we didn't behave," I told Connor with a smile.

"How are the guitar lessons going?" he asked me.

"Good," I replied. "How about you? I haven't seen you at Mrs. Minerva's lately." Mrs. Minerva was our extremely strict guitar teacher.

"I had to change my lesson time," he said. I wondered if Selena had made him do that so he wouldn't run into me, but I dismissed the notion as egotistical. Besides, Selena, a budding sorceress, would probably put a spell on anyone who looked twice at her boyfriend.

After Connor took our order, I looked for Flo so I could give her a report.

I found her filling water glasses behind the counter.

Her T-shirt read I'M YOUR WORST NIGHTMARE. Flo's bad attitude had decreased only an infinitesimal amount since she'd gotten married to Vinnie, the drummer for Side Effects May Vary.

"We saw a demon horse at the beach the other night," I said.

"I know," she replied. "Andy already told me." Figures. Andy was Flo's pet.

"Ever heard of anything like that?"

She shook her head. "I'll ask Lydia about it." Dominic and Raven's mom was now the most experienced virago in town.

I had been dismissed, but I stood there. Flo wasn't going to like what else I had to tell her.

"Anything else?" she asked.

"I have to miss practice on Wednesday," I said. "Mom's making us take horse-riding lessons and I can't get out of it."

I expected her to scold me, but she said, "Horse riding, huh? Where?"

"Phantasm Farms," I replied.

"Could be useful."

I waited, but she didn't elaborate, so I headed back.

I stopped by the kitchen to say hi to Slim. "How's married life?" I asked him.

A few months ago, everyone had been hopeful that Slim would stop being invisible and return to normal. Unfortunately, he'd kind of frozen midway. The left side of his face was back, but the rest remained invisible.

His wife, Natalie, didn't mind, but Slim did. He had wanted to be visible for the wedding. "For once, I'd like a good photo," he had joked. "I haven't had one since my high school graduation."

I wanted to ask Flo how Slim had become invisible in the first place, but I wasn't sure she'd tell me. It was more likely that she'd tell me to mind my own business.

The wedding had been beautiful anyway.

"Married life is amazing," Slim said. "Natalie is amazing." The gooey look in his one good eye convinced me it was time to return to my table, so I said goodbye.

"What did I miss?" I asked Eva, whose eyes were glazing over. Dominic and Evan were deep in conversation.

"Nothing much," she said. "They're debating the world's fastest runner's time or something equally thrilling."

Our boyfriends were both on the Nightshade High track team.

"It's nice they have something in common," I said.

"It would be nicer if my boyfriend paid some attention to me," she said.

Evan looked up with a distracted air. "What did you say?"

Eva laughed. "Never mind."

He scooted closer to her. "Have I been neglecting you? Sorry."

She leaned in for a kiss. "You're forgiven."

Connor came back with our food and I took a giant bite of my burger. "I'm starving."

Dominic leaned over and snagged a fry. "Did you run this morning?"

"Not today," I replied. "Flo canceled, so Eva came over." Flo usually made all the viragoes go for a long run every Saturday. "What did you do?"

What I hoped he'd say was that he had said goodbye to his ex-girlfriend, but instead he shrugged. "Nothing much."

"So she's still here?"

"Who's still here?" Evan asked. Eva elbowed him in the ribs.

"Dominic's ex-girlfriend is staying at his house," I said.

"Don't make it sound like that," Dominic objected.

"It's true," I snapped.

"C'mon, Evan," Eva said. "Let's put a quarter in the jukebox." She was making an exit so Dominic and I could fight.

Rumor was that the jukebox used to be possessed, but local psychic Daisy Giordano had exorcised it somehow. It was just a regular jukebox now. I kind of missed its old unpredictable ways. It used to play "The Warrior" every time I stepped into Slim's.

"Why is she here in the first place?" I demanded.

He hesitated. "To see me."

"That's just great."

"We're just friends, Jess."

"How long is she staying with you?" I asked.

"She's not staying at Aunt Katrina's. There isn't enough room, but even if there were, I'd want her to leave."

"You would?"

"Of course," he said. "I know it would make you as uncomfortable as it would make me. She's staying at Harmony's."

"She knows Harmony Clare?"

"Their moms are old friends," he said. "Now can we stop talking about Tashya and enjoy the rest of the night?"

I nodded but my tattoo tingled, and I couldn't figure

out why. It wasn't exactly a tattoo, because the whirlwind moved sometimes, but I didn't know what else to call it. When the weird mark had appeared on my arm, my life had changed. Maybe it was about to change again.

CHAPTER THREE

Eva and I met at the bus stop before school the first day. "I figured Dominic might pick you up," she said.

I bumped her shoulder with mine. "There's no way I was going to miss our first-day-of-school ritual."

She whipped out her handheld video camera and pointed it at me. "Smile!"

"No way," I replied. "You get in here too." I draped an arm around her and dragged her closer.

Eva did her usual commentary with the date, time, etc. Only this time, she felt compelled to add something about the current state of our love lives.

I tried to wrestle the camera away from her. "That's enough of that."

"What's the matter? Don't you want the world to know you're dating a future rock god?"

"Everyone in Nightshade already knows," I reminded her.

"Like Dominic will stay in Nightshade for long," she said, then saw my face. "Sorry. I didn't mean it."

I shrugged. "It's true. He's bound to leave."

Eva gave me a hug. "I didn't mean to depress you," she said. "Going back to school is depressing enough. How much do you want to bet that Mr. Krayson assigns homework on the first day?"

I wasn't taking that bet. Mr. Krayson was Nightshade High's least popular teacher and Eva and I both had him for first period.

The first day of school went smoothly, but the teachers didn't bother to ease us back into things. I had a pile of homework already and not just in Mr. Krayson's class.

At the end of the day, Raven, Eva, and I walked to chorus together. There was a bulletin board outside the music room and Eva went over to check it.

She came back with a red and gold flyer in her hand. "A circus is coming to town," she said.

"I don't like seeing the animals in cages," Raven said.

"Me, neither," I replied.

"I don't like the clowns," Eva said.

"Me, neither," I said again.

We all giggled.

"So we're definitely going, then?" Eva asked.

"I don't see how I'll be able to get out of it," I admitted. "At least not once my little sisters find out about it."

In the music room, Dominic was surrounded by his fans as usual, but when he saw me, he broke free to say hi.

Our choir director, Ms. Clare, was super-strict about public displays of affection, so I had to be happy with just holding Dom's hand.

"How was your first day?" he asked.

"Tons of homework," I told him. "You?"

"Me, too," he said. "I thought the teachers might go easy on us senior year."

"Settle down, everyone," Ms. Clare said. "Let's get started."

We obediently took our places.

"We don't have much time before our first performance," Ms. Clare continued.

"When is that?" Harmony asked.

"I'm glad you asked," her mom replied. "There will be a Day of the Dead party at the Wilder estate, and the choir has been invited to perform. Now who has suggestions for Halloween-themed songs?"

"How about 'Monster Mash'?" Connor suggested.

"How about something from the last decade?" Selena teased.

"Like what?" Ms. Clare challenged.

That stumped Selena for a few seconds. "What about an a cappella version of 'This Is Halloween'?"

The suggestions flew and Ms. Clare wrote them all down on the board. "One of the numbers will be a duet," she said. "So think about your audition piece. It should reflect the theme."

I hoped Dominic would ask me to audition with him, but he didn't say anything before I left to meet the other viragoes.

Raven, Andy, and I had arranged to meet by the oak tree in the front of the school. Eva walked with me. "Are you going to audition with Dominic?" she asked.

I shrugged. Dominic and I had performed a duet with Side Effects May Vary at the Battle of the Bands but hadn't sung together since then. I wondered if the other band members didn't like me horning in on their gig.

"I need to swing by the library," I told Andy. She had her license, so she usually drove me and Raven around.

"Me, too," she said. "I can't believe how much homework I already have."

My favorite librarian, Ms. Johns, was manning the front desk when we arrived. She looked like she'd been crying.

"What's wrong, Ms. Johns?" I asked her. "Allergies?" I thought I'd give her an out if my question was too nosy.

She shook her head. "I guess you haven't heard the news yet," she said. "Mrs. Lincoln died last night." Mrs. Lincoln had been one of the older librarians, but she wasn't *that* old.

Raven gasped. "What happened?"

"Nobody really knows," Ms. Johns replied. "She lived alone. She didn't show up for work today, so I went to check on her."

"I'm so sorry," I said. "You don't have to talk about it if you don't want to."

"No, I do," she said. "It was just so strange. The look on her face. It looked like she died screaming."

"Screaming?" Andy asked. "That's odd."

"I know, right?" Ms. Johns said, sniffling.

"Then what happened?" I asked.

"I called the police and they took over. Deputy Denton wanted to drive me home, but I didn't want to be alone, so I came here."

"How do they think she died?" Raven asked.

"They think she was murdered. There were signs that she was smothered."

"That's horrible. Is there anything we can do?" I asked.

"No, I think it's being handled already," she replied. "Mrs. Lincoln had a nephew, but I haven't been able to get in touch with him."

"I'm so sorry," I said again.

After we left, Andy said, "Do you think Mrs. Lincoln's death has something to do with the horse on the beach?"

"Maybe it's just a coincidence," I said. "But my tattoo did tingle when we saw it. And then someone was murdered right after we saw that ghostly horse."

Raven held up the stack of books she'd checked out. "I'm about to find out what that was all about." She read aloud while Andy drove.

"Here it is," she said finally. "A supernatural horse called a night mare is also known as a Mara. A Mara gallops into someone's dreams. Even a glimpse of the deadly Mara is enough to scare some people to death."

"How can we stop it?" I asked.

"It doesn't say," she said.

"That's not good," Andy grumbled. Understatement of the year.

CHAPTER **FOUR**

My little sisters Katie and Kellie had their first riding lesson after school on Wednesday. Mom had roped me into going too, but since I didn't have my driver's license yet, she was paying our next-door neighbor Poppy Giordano, Daisy's sister, to take us. In fact, Poppy was running the ultimate kids' chauffeur service in between her classes at UC Nightshade. She picked my sisters up from school and then drove them all over town for their various activities when Dad and Mom couldn't make it.

When Poppy arrived, Kellie was eating a snack in the kitchen, but there was no sign of Katie.

"Katie, Poppy's here," I called, but she didn't answer. I was pretty sure she was upstairs playing with her dollhouse. Normally, playing with a dollhouse wouldn't be worrisome, but Katie's was enchanted. We'd discovered it in the old Mason house, and Natalie had given it to my sister. The dollhouse was amazing, a miniature medieval castle, like something straight out of a fairy tale.

Princess Antonia, the main occupant of the doll-house, was a royal pain in the butt.

I walked up the stairs to Katie's room. She was having a conversation with Princess Antonia. "I don't think Jessica will like it," Katie said.

The princess, who had a very loud voice for a little doll that had come to life, said something I couldn't catch.

"All right," Katie reluctantly agreed. "I'll do it."

"You'll do what?" I asked.

Katie and the princess both jumped about a foot.

I leaned in and gave Princess Antonia a stern glare. "Do not get my sister into trouble," I said, "or you will regret it."

She shrugged and turned back to her gilt-framed mirror. "I have no idea what you are speaking of."

"Yeah, right," I said. "I mean it, or I'm going to have to have a talk with the prince."

"The prince," she sniffed.

Sounded like trouble in miniature paradise, but I didn't have time to worry about the royal relationship right then.

"Katie, are you ready?" I asked. "Poppy's here. Make sure you wear the boots Mom bought you."

She put out a leg and admired her new riding boots. "I'm ready."

We found Kellie downstairs, tugging on her boots. We piled into the car.

"Jessica, not that I mind the extra cash, but isn't it almost time for you to be driving by now?" Poppy asked.

I nodded. "I just got my learner's permit," I explained. "I still have six months before I turn sixteen."

"What made your mom decide on riding lessons, anyway?"

I shrugged. "She was the Realtor who sold Phantasm Farms to the new owner," I said. "Have you ever been out there?"

"We went a few times when I was little," Poppy said. "The place is huge. There's the stables, of course, but there's also a couple of barns, pastures for all the horses, and the original house, which was deserted. The last owners built a huge new house but left the old one alone."

"Why would they do that?"

Poppy shrugged. "Everyone said it was haunted."

I glanced back at my sisters, but they were busy staring out the window at all the horses in the pasture.

"We're here," I said.

Poppy nodded. "Kind of," she said. She pointed to a sign that read PHANTASM FARMS. "We turn up that lane and then the stables are still about a mile away."

"Yikes," I said. "No wonder Mom didn't think we could walk."

"Here we are," Poppy said. "I'll meet you guys in about an hour." She pointed to a picnic table under a shade tree. "Wait here if I'm late." She let us out and we headed to the stables, where a short blond man in jeans, checkered shirt, and a black hat was waiting for us.

"Hi. We're the Walsh kids," I said.

"Anton Plasky," he replied. "Let's get you saddled up."

We were on the horses in a matter of minutes. Katie and Kellie had placid old ponies, but my horse looked like he wanted to take a bite out of me.

"Buttercup can tell you're afraid," Mr. Platsky said. "He has to know you are in command."

I held the reins a little more firmly, which seemed to help, but I was still nervous.

We rode around the farm until some of my skittishness evaporated.

The horses carried us along a trail leading into the woods. Katie was in the lead when her horse veered off course and went crashing through the brush.

"Katie!" I cried.

"Wait here," Mr. Platsky commanded, and took off after her.

There was no way I was going to just sit there. "C'mon," I said to Kellie. "But be careful."

We followed them at a more sedate pace. Whatever had spooked Katie's horse seemed to be gone now, because Buttercup plodded along, and stopped to chew grass as he went.

We caught up to them near a dilapidated old house. It must have been the one Poppy had told us about. It looked like something out of one of Eva's favorite horror movies.

"Look, Jessica, it's the haunted house," Katie said. "Can we go in?"

"It's not haunted," I assured her. "Just deserted."

"But I saw a ghost," she replied. "A girl in a white dress. Up there." She pointed to an upper-story window.

"There's nobody there," I said.

"Lesson's over," Mr. Platsky snapped.

He hurried us back to the stable. He and my sisters had already led their horses to the barn while I was trudging along. As I dismounted, I landed wrong on my left foot and it twisted hard. I tried to stand, but it hurt too much. The ankle was swelling rapidly.

"Hello? Mr. Platsky? Help!" I yelled, but there wasn't any answer.

Even my horse abandoned me. He smelled oats and headed for the barn door, leaving me lying on the ground.

There was a flash of white and then a blond girl in a white dress appeared, peeking out from behind a barn door. "Hey, can you help me?" I yelled. "I twisted my ankle."

The sound of my voice made her jump. She shied away and looked around fearfully, but when she saw I was alone, she crept closer. Kellie had said she saw a girl in white in the abandoned house. Could she really be a ghost? There was only one way to find out. I reached out to her.

"Can you help me stand?" I asked. "Please?"

She inched closer. The girl's dress was faded and torn along the hem and her hair was a mass of tangles. Her skin was so pale I could almost see through it.

"What's your name?" I held out my hand again, but she backed away. "I won't hurt you," I added. "My name is Jessica."

"Sanja," she whispered.

She helped me up with a hand that was warm and very real. Not a ghost, then. I leaned on her until we made it to the stable door. Sanja was shaking so badly she could barely walk.

"It's okay," I soothed.

"Jessica," Mr. Platsky barked from the barn. "What's taking you so long?"

The girl bolted. By the time Mr. Platsky had reached the yard, she was long gone.

"Who were you talking to?" he asked suspiciously.

"I was yelling for help," I said. "I twisted my ankle."

"Where is Buttercup?"

"He headed for the barn," I said.

Mr. Platsky left me where I stood and rushed off after his steed. Kellie and Katie came out of the barn soon afterward.

"Jessica, what happened?" Kellie asked.

"I'm fine," I replied. "I just twisted my ankle. Can you help me?"

Standing on either side of me, my sisters supported me while I limped over to the picnic table. I called Mom. "I think I sprained my ankle," I told her.

"Have Poppy take you to Dr. Joyce's," she ordered. "Your dad and I will meet you there."

When Poppy arrived, she helped me to the van. "Buckle up," she said, "and put this on your ankle." She handed me a Ziploc bag of ice.

"Did Mom call you?" I asked.

"No, Rose told me to bring it," she said. "Now I know why."

Rose? Then I remembered that Poppy's sister was telepathic.

After what I considered to be too much fussing, the doctor confirmed that it was a bad sprain and wrote me an excuse note to skip soccer. I'd have to make a copy for Flo, since I'd probably have to miss a couple of weeks of virago training, too.

CHAPTER FIVE

Mom made me stay home from school the next day. I spent the entire time reading in my room with some comfort food for sustenance. It was the longest I'd sat still in years. I even dozed off for a couple of hours from boredom.

I was relieved when Eva came to visit me after school.

"How's the invalid?" she asked.

"Bored out of my mind," I told her. "Amuse me. What happened at school today?"

"Nothing much." She brightened. "We did get a new art teacher."

"It's not creepy artist guy, is it? Jensen Kenton?"

She made a face. "Hardly," she replied. "Mr. Martin is cute and young. And he carves these amazing marionettes out of pieces of scrap wood. Remember the ones at the library? Those are his. We're even carving our own marionettes in his class. He's so talented."

"Does Evan have to worry?" I asked.

She giggled. "Gross. There's nothing creepier than having a crush on a teacher. Unless it's a teacher having a crush on a student."

"Just checking," I said.

"Anyway, I can't stay long," Eva said. "I've got to submit a sketch for my marionette by Monday."

She handed me a stack of homework.

I groaned.

Mom knocked on the door. "Jessica, you have another visitor," she said. "Are you decent?"

I hadn't combed my hair all day and I probably had Cheetos breath. "Just a minute," I called.

"Hand me my crutches," I whispered to Eva.

"Why?"

"Because Mom never asks if I'm decent unless it's a boy. It's probably Dominic."

Eva followed me to the sink and I brushed my teeth and combed my hair, and then swapped the ratty T-shirt I'd been wearing for something more attractive.

"All clear," I called.

My boyfriend entered the room. "Raven told me you sprained your ankle," he said. "So I thought I'd bring you something to cheer you up." He was holding a bunch of balloons.

"I just remembered I was supposed to meet Evan,"

Eva said. She jumped off my bed and headed out the door before I could say anything.

Dominic looked after her in amusement. "Was it something I said?"

"She was trying to give us some privacy," I told him.

He bent down to kiss me, which made me glad I had brushed my teeth. "I like that idea."

"Enjoy it while you can," I said. "Because Katie will be in here within seconds."

My prediction came true when my sister bounded into the room. "Dominic, I'm glad you're here to visit me," she said.

Dominic and Katie were great friends. He gave me a charming smile when she led him away to look at her dollhouse. "We'll be back," he said.

A few minutes later, I heard Katie shouting. I grabbed my crutches and hobbled down the hall to see what was wrong.

"The princess is missing," she said.

"She's probably just in a snit and hiding somewhere," I told her.

"We'll find her," Dominic said soothingly. "I promise."

We looked all over, but Princess Antonia had vanished.

Mom interrupted our search by asking, "Dominic, would you like to stay for dinner?"

"I'd love to," he replied. "Raven's at Andy's and Aunt Katrina is out with her boyfriend." He tried not to make a face when he said the last part. To everyone's surprise, Katrina was still dating Brett, the terrible lead singer of a band called Hamlin.

The search for the princess was called off for now. Katie led Dominic off to play cards in the living room while I helped with dinner.

I was sitting at the counter chopping vegetables for the salad while Mom cooked the rice. Dad was outside barbecuing chicken while Grace and Kellie played tag and Fiona finished her homework. I wasn't sure what Sarah and Sydney were doing, besides avoiding work. I tried to pump my mom for information about the new residents of Phantasm Farms.

"There's a little girl there named Sanja," I said.

"Sanja is Anton Platsky's daughter," Mom said. "He mentioned her the first time he looked at the listing."

"Katie and Kellie say they haven't seen her at school," I said.

"Maybe she's homeschooled," Mom replied.

"Maybe," I said. "She seemed . . . untamed."

"What do you mean?"

"It was like she didn't even know how to talk to people."

"She's great with the horses, though," Mom said.

"She's won blue medals and a whole room of trophies. Mr. Platsky showed them to me once. He's very proud of her."

That didn't sound like the Mr. Platsky I'd met.

"She was scared, Mom," I said flatly.

"Of what?"

"I don't know."

"Maybe I should cancel your lessons," Mom fretted.

"No, don't do that!" I said. "I'll keep Kellie and Katie safe."

"You're a good big sister," she replied.

I would keep them safe, but I also wanted an excuse to snoop around Phantasm Farms.

Sydney and Sarah finally came into the kitchen. Sarah was a high school freshman and Sydney was in eighth grade, but they were inseparable most of the time.

"Nice of you to show up now that all the work is done," I said sourly.

"Ignore her," Sarah said to Sydney. "She's just worried because her hot boyfriend's hot ex showed up."

I glared at her. "I'm not worried. And keep it down. Dominic's in the next room with Katie."

Sarah lowered her voice but kept talking. "I heard Bethany Harris talking in study hall. She said that Tashya's been hanging out at the band's rehearsals."

Mom overheard her. "Bethany Harris never just talks,

she gossips. It's not an attractive trait. Sarah, you would do well to remember that. Now I want you and Sydney to go set the table."

I was hurt, even though Bethany, Eva's sister, had never been very friendly. To me or Eva.

Mom waited to grill me until my sisters had left the room. "Is everything okay, Jessica?"

"Everything's fine, Mom," I said. "Dominic is here, remember? And since when do you listen to gossip, anyway?"

That shut her up, but it didn't stop me from thinking about what Sarah had said. Tashya had been at band rehearsal? I didn't like the sound of that one bit.

I didn't have much hope of getting any alone time with my boyfriend, but after dinner, Mom rounded up all of my sisters and took them out for ice cream.

"Do you want me to help you to your room?" Dominic asked when they were gone.

I laughed. "Not if you want to live." No one of the opposite sex in our rooms when my parents weren't home. Of course, my brother, Sean, who managed to get the only bedroom on the first floor, had somehow been exempt from the rule. Or my parents never realized how many times Samantha had snuck in through his window.

"The living room it is, then," Dominic said. He picked me up in his arms.

"Dom, put me down!"

"I will," he said. "Eventually."

He settled me on the couch and then propped up my ankle with a bunch of pillows.

"You're good at taking care of me."

He sat next to me and put his arm around me. "I try."

We watched television in comfortable silence. "Hey, Jessica," he finally said.

"Yes?"

"Tashya's been to one rehearsal," he said. "And I told her not to come again."

"You heard Sarah?"

He nodded. "I'm sorry. I think Tashya finally gets it now."

"Gets what?"

"That I'm crazy about you," he said. His kiss confirmed it.

By the time my family came back, I felt a lot more confident that Tashya wasn't going to come between me and Dominic, no matter how hard she tried.

CHAPTER SIX

The news spread around Nightshade High that there had been another murder. This time it was Tad Collins, a professor at the local college, UC Nightshade. He'd been found in his bedroom with his mouth stuffed full of cockroaches.

We were eating lunch when the subject came up. I pushed away my tray when I heard the details.

"That's just gross," Raven said.

"It sounds like something out of a horror movie," Eva said.

"Or a nightmare." I handed Eva my chips. "I want to take another look at Jensen Kenton's artwork."

Raven shuddered theatrically. "Why?"

"Tad Collins's murder reminds me of one of his paintings."

"Do you think you should be walking on your ankle so much?" Eva asked.

"I have crutches if I need them, but my ankle is a lot better," I said.

"I'll drive," Andy offered. "Meet me at my car as soon as school is over."

The lunchroom dismissal bell rang and Raven grabbed my tray. "I'll take it. You head for class. We'll catch up."

It was true that they would catch up. My twisted ankle made me about as fast as Kellie's pet turtle.

"Jessica, wait up," Dominic called out. "I'll walk you to class." He grabbed my backpack, and I noticed Tashya staring at us as we passed her locker. I stared back.

"I didn't see you at lunch today," I said to Dom.

"Chess club meeting," he said. "Evan convinced me to join."

"Chess, huh? I didn't know you know how to play."

"I don't," he replied. "But I thought I'd learn so I'll have something to pass the time on the road."

I tried to pretend the mention of his tour didn't bother me. "I'm glad you'll have something to keep you busy."

"So what song are we going to do for our duet?"

"Are you asking me to audition with you?" He'd taken long enough. Dominic was quick to catch the miffed tone in my voice.

"I've been meaning to ask you," he said. "But I just as-

43

sumed . . ." He trailed off, probably realizing he was only making it worse.

I finally took pity on him and laughed. "I was just kidding," I said. "Do you have any ideas?"

"A few. Want to get together after school?"

"I can't," I said. "Virago stuff."

We'd reached my classroom. "I'll call you tonight, then." He gave me a quick kiss right before the teacher got there.

"Mr. Gray, this is sophomore English," Ms. Miller said.

"Just helping Jessica," Dominic said.

I stuck out my bum ankle and tried to look helpless.

"Fine," she said. "But the tardy bell will ring in approximately two minutes, so I suggest you get to class."

After school, I hobbled out to the parking lot. I was the first one there but knew better than to lean against Andy's car. She loved that car like it was a person.

I set my crutches on the ground and sat on the curb and waited. I was out of sight, but I was enjoying the sun on my face.

That was, until I heard Selena, Harmony, and Tashya talking. I peeked out and saw Connor and Noel trailing behind their girlfriends.

"Don't you think you were kind of obvious just now?"

Harmony asked. "Dominic seemed really uncomfortable. And he has a girlfriend."

"You think that was obvious?" Tashya replied. "I haven't even gotten started yet. And I have a plan for that little girlfriend of his." Her screechy laugh set my nerves on edge.

Connor cleared his throat nervously. "Jessica's a friend of mine, Tashya. Leave her alone."

I thought for sure Selena would get ticked off at Connor coming to my defense, but instead, she chimed in. "Connor's right, Tashya. Jessica and Dominic are our friends, so leave us out of whatever you're planning."

"Don't worry, I will," Tashya snapped. "I don't need any help to take care of Jessica Walsh."

They got into Connor's car and drove away without seeing me. But I had a feeling it wouldn't have mattered if they had. Tashya didn't care who knew she was after Dominic.

The other v-girls finally showed up and we headed to the library.

The community room where the exhibit hung was closed.

"What now?" Raven asked.

"Let's see if Ms. Johns is working," I said.

We found her at the reference desk. "Ms. Johns, we

need a favor," I said. "We need to take a look at some of the paintings in the exhibit."

"It's open," she said. "Until seven tonight."

I shook my head. "The door was locked."

She frowned. "That can't be right. Let me get my keys."

We walked back together to the door of the community room and Ms. Johns turned the handle to get inside. When she realized that the room was indeed locked up tight, she took out her keys and unlocked the door. We followed her inside.

Ms. Johns went from aisle to aisle checking on the paintings.

"I don't think anything is missing, but I'll check the sales list," she said.

We were heading back from the far end of the room when a guy stepped out of the shadows and nearly ran into us.

"Mr. Martin!" Ms. Johns exclaimed as she skidded to a stop. "You scared me."

I thought he'd had something in his hands, but he put them in his pockets, so I couldn't tell for sure. "Nice to see you again," he said, giving the librarian a charming smile.

"The door was locked," Andy said. "How did you get in here?"

He shrugged. "It was open when I got here."

Ms. Johns frowned. "I'm so sorry. You could have been stuck in here all night."

"But I wasn't," he said. Mr. Martin was in his late twenties or early thirties. He was handsome, with untamed curly brown hair and deep brown eyes.

He held out his hand to me. It was stained with paint. When he saw me staring at the stain, he took out a rag from his back pocket and wiped it off. "Javier Martin," he said. "I'm the new art teacher at Nightshade High. I was just doing some touchup work on one of my babies." He gestured to a group of princess marionettes in pastel ball gowns. They all had sparkling sapphire eyes and perfect, painted-on smiles.

I leaned on my crutches to take his hand. "Jessica Walsh," I said. "And this is Andy Rudolph and Raven Gray. We all go to Nightshade."

"Nice to meet you all," he said. "Now if you'll excuse me, I really must be going."

Ms. Johns walked with him to the exit. I stared after them until Andy nudged me. "Isn't there a painting you wanted to look at?"

"You're right," I said. "I think it's this way."

"It's not here," Andy said, after we'd gone through the exhibit again.

"There's probably a catalog around here somewhere," Raven suggested. "We can double-check."

I spotted some brochures by the entrance and leafed through one. Every painting in the exhibit had a description and a photo.

In the brochure, I finally found the Jensen Kenton painting of a mouth full of cockroaches. "This is it."

"This is what you wanted us to see?" Raven asked.

"Yes, remember, Tad Collins was found just like this. Dead and his mouth full of cockroaches. It can't be a coincidence."

"What about Mrs. Lincoln?" Andy asked. "If your theory is true, then there should be a painting that relates to her death, too."

"Good point," I said. "I don't remember one, but let's look."

We searched the entire exhibit a third time but didn't find a painting that matched the details of the old librarian's death.

CHAPTER SEVEN

Once back home, I elevated my ankle and planned to lounge for the rest of the night.

But then the doorbell rang.

Daisy Giordano stood there with a plate of cookies. "Hi, Jessica," she said. "I've been practicing my baking skills and we have way too many cookies left. I thought you guys might like them."

"We'd love some," I said. "Come on in and tell me what you've been up to lately, besides baking. How's Ryan?"

Daisy winked at me. "He's just fine." When I was younger, I had a huge crush on Daisy's boyfriend, Ryan Mendez. He was my brother's best friend and totally gorgeous besides.

"What kind of cookies are they?" I asked.

"Sugar skull cookies," she said. "I'm working on a new frosting recipe for the Day of the Dead party at the Wilders'." The Wilder estate, with stone walls, intimidating décor, and five-star restaurant, would be the perfect place for the spooky theme party. Daisy took cooking lessons from the head chef there.

"Sounds like it'll be fun."

"The whole town is coming," she replied. "The Nightshade City Council is sponsoring the event."

Daisy pried open the Tupperware lid and showed me the rows of meticulously decorated skeletons. We sat at the kitchen counter dipping the cookies into cold glasses of milk.

"Dominic's band is playing the party," I said. Then I took the conversation in a darker direction. I knew that Daisy had investigated lots of unusual doings in Nightshade, so I asked, "Have you heard about the murders?"

"I heard," she said. "Ryan overheard Chief Wells say that Tad Collins had garnets all over his apartment." Ryan was a police trainee.

"Was he a geology professor?" I asked. Daisy was a student at UC Nightshade, where Tad Collins had taught.

"No, he was an art history teacher," she said. "But garnets are supposed to be protection against nightmares."

Sadly, those good luck charms hadn't worked.

"Did you pick up on anything on campus, psychically speaking?" I asked. "Or maybe Rose?" Daisy and her sisters, Poppy and Rose, all had psychic abilities.

"Nothing. You?"

I shook my head. "I saw a ghostly white horse on the beach one night, and then the next night Mrs. Lincoln was dead."

Daisy frowned. "I don't know if a horse could kill her, but it probably couldn't rob her."

"What do you mean?"

"Ryan told me in confidence that lots of valuables were stolen from Mrs. Lincoln's house," Daisy said. "Like jewelry and cash."

"Maybe she walked in on them and they killed her? Or they were scared off before they could finish the robbery? Though I hate to think anyone in Nightshade would be capable of that," I said.

Daisy took a bite of her cookie. "Who's new in town?"

"The owner of Phantasm Farms," I told her. "And that guy Jensen Kenton, who has a bunch of creepy paintings on display at the library."

"Those paintings are supposedly worth a lot," she said, "creepy as they are. Which is why it's also odd that whoever killed Professor Collins didn't steal the Kenton painting he owned."

I gulped. I bet I could guess which one it was. What I couldn't guess was whether the killer had just copied the gruesome scene in the painting, or if the painting itself was somehow to blame for Tad Collins's death.

I took a bite of my cookie and nearly swooned. "Daisy, this frosting is amazing."

"Thanks," she said. She looked at our kitchen clock. "I've got to get back. Chef Pierre is going to show me how to make his secret-recipe ganache next."

"I'll walk you out," I said.

"Not with your sprained ankle," she said.

But the doorbell rang again. "Stay put," she said. "I'll answer it."

She came back to the kitchen with Ryan Mendez in tow. Ryan seemed to get better looking every time I saw him. His summer tan only made his green eyes look more intense. He still made my heart beat a little faster. Not as fast as Dominic did, though.

"I was hoping to catch you here," he said.

"I'll leave you two alone, then," I said. I started to walk upstairs, but Ryan stopped me.

"Jessica, I was talking about you."

The surprise on my face must have been comical, because Daisy and Ryan burst out laughing.

"I wanted to know if you'd heard from Sean lately," he said to me. "He isn't answering my texts."

I shrugged. "I haven't. But I'm only his sister. Have you talked to Samantha?"

Besides being my brother's girlfriend, Samantha Devereaux was Daisy's best friend. When I was a freshman, my main goal had been to be as popular as Sam was in high school.

"Samantha isn't returning my calls either," Ryan replied.

"I haven't heard from her in a few days," Daisy said.

"I'll ask my parents to track Sean down," I said.

"Thanks, Jessica," Ryan said. "I'm worried about him."

"You know Sean," I said. "He's probably caught up in football, or maybe even actual classes."

Ryan and Daisy said their goodbyes, but the conversation troubled me.

At dinner, I decided to see if my parents had heard from Sean. Without freaking them out, of course. He was their only son. Mom would probably drive to his college in Orange County straightaway if she thought there might be anything wrong.

"Now that you mention it," Mom said. "I haven't heard from Sean in days."

My brother might blow off his family, but he and Ryan were close. It wasn't like him not to keep in touch.

I sent Sean a text, but didn't get a reply. I was starting to get worried too.

CHAPTER EIGHT

Since I was still out of commission because of my ankle, I didn't have to run on Saturday, but I did have to babysit Katie while Mom and Dad did errands.

"Jessica, I'm going to the grocery store with Kellie and Grace," Mom said. "Do you need anything?"

"Can you pick me up a brush and some detangler?" I asked. "It's a present for Sanja. That mane of hers looks like she's been using a horse brush on it."

"That's thoughtful of you," Mom replied. "Her mother has been dead since she was a baby. Her father mentioned he was baffled by girls. I'm sure it isn't easy on either of them."

Dominic picked up Katie and me and we met Eva at Slim's.

She looked exhausted and immediately ordered a coffee and a large soda.

"What's the matter with you?" I asked as she dropped into the booth next to me.

"Nice to see you, too," she replied. "I think I need to cut back on the VP movies."

"What? You love Vincent Price."

"I know," she said. "But I've been having weird dreams. I can barely get any sleep."

"What kinds of dreams?"

"How long has this been going on?" Dominic asked.

Eva stared at us. "Why the sudden interest in my sleeping habits?"

"Something or someone is haunting people's dreams," I said. "And we're trying to stop them. So tell us everything you can remember."

She shrugged. "It's always the same dream," she said. "It starts out calm. Beautiful, even."

"And then?" I asked.

"And then I wake up screaming," she said.

"You don't remember anything in between?" asked Dominic.

She concentrated. "Not much," she said. "I've been trying to forget." She trembled. "But there is one thing. I remember hearing the sound of someone or something running. Something big."

"Could it have been an animal galloping?" I inquired.

"You mean like the white horse we saw?" Eva knew the plot to every horror movie ever made, so it didn't take her long to make the connection. "Maybe."

"What does Flo think about the whole night terrors thing?" Dominic asked me.

I shrugged. "She seems preoccupied."

"Why do you say that?" Eva asked.

"I don't know," I said. "She doesn't really seem into it these days."

"Do you think she'll retire?" Eva asked. Andy had told me once that Flo would retire from being a virago after getting married. Was Flo going to leave us?

Dominic reached over and grabbed one of my fries. "Flo? Retire? That's like saying my mom will retire." There was a trace of bitterness in his voice.

Tashya and her new best friend, Harmony, walked in and took a table across from us. As much as I hated to admit it, Tashya was gorgeous.

"Perfect," Dominic muttered.

"When is she supposed to leave?" I asked.

Tashya overheard me and came over. "Didn't Dominic tell you? I'm staying."

"Staying?" I pushed away my food. "Since when?"

"Your parents let you transfer schools?" Dominic asked. He looked almost as sick as I felt.

"You know my parents travel a lot, Dom. I'm staying with Harmony for the rest of the school year." She sashayed back to her table and she and Harmony burst into loud laughter.

"Did you know about this?" I asked Dominic.

"She mentioned it in English lit," he said. "But I never thought her parents would go for it."

"Well, obviously, they did," I replied. Dominic caught the edge in my voice.

"Ignore her," he said. "That's what I plan to do."

"She's in half your classes. Pretty hard to ignore that."

"Try," he said. "For me?"

I couldn't resist him when he looked at me that way. "I'll try."

He changed the subject. "Making any progress on the case?"

I shook my head. "None. I don't suppose you've come across any clues as songs?"

"Sorry, I've been sticking to the set list lately."

Eva's tired eyes widened. I looked up and saw the last person I expected to see walking through the door of Slim's.

"Sean!" Katie screeched, and got up to hug our big brother.

"Sean, what are you doing home?" Eva asked. "Not that we aren't glad to see you."

"You look awful," I said. "What happened?" My brother's eyes were red-rimmed and weary and his clothes looked like he'd been wearing them for a couple of days at least.

"Sam's in the hospital," he said. "Unconscious. I just took a break to come by to tell you."

Eva gasped. "Is she going to be okay?"

"They don't know," Sean said.

"What can we do to help?" I asked.

"I honestly don't know," he said. My big bad brother looked like he was about to cry.

While everyone crowded around him for details, Katie stood apart. Tears rolled down her face. Katie loved Samantha, maybe even more than she loved Dominic.

I kneeled down beside her. "Samantha is going to be okay," I said.

Katie crossed her arms. "How do you know? You're not psychic."

"No, I'm not," I admitted. "But I know someone who is. We'll go find Daisy." The beginning of an idea was stirring in my brain.

"Can you go without me?" Sean asked. "I want to get back to the hospital."

"Of course." I reached in for a brief hug, but he hugged me back hard.

Dominic dropped off Katie and me at home. "Sorry, but I've got to leave for a gig," he said. "I'll be in San Francisco overnight, but call me tomorrow and let me know how Sam is."

I gave him a goodbye kiss and then hobbled over to the Giordano house.

Daisy was home and I told her the news about Sam. "Why didn't Sean call us?" she asked.

"He didn't call anyone," I told her. "He's completely freaked out."

"I'm going to the hospital right now," she said. "Want to come along?"

I nodded. "In fact, I have this crazy idea."

When Daisy heard what I was thinking, she made me think my idea might not be so crazy after all.

"Sean said the doctors have no idea how it happened," I explained.

"But you do?" Daisy guessed.

"I think it has something to do with nightmares," I said. "And the murders. I think someone is sending nightmares to do their dirty work. People are dying of fear."

"How can I help?"

"I don't want you to do anything risky," I said. "But I think maybe if you could make a psychic connection with Samantha, you could figure out exactly what happened."

"I'll try," Daisy promised.

"And I'll be there, just in case anything goes wrong."

She smiled. "What could go wrong as long as a virago has my back?"

When we got to the hospital, Sam's room was empty of visitors.

"Her mom didn't even bother to show up," Daisy said angrily.

I motioned to a huge floral arrangement. "It looks like she sent flowers."

"Samantha hates roses," she retorted. "She thinks they're pedestrian."

She noticed my startled look. "Sorry, I wasn't snapping at you."

"I know," I replied. "I'm just here and Sam's mom isn't."

Daisy stared down at her friend. "No wonder Sean was so upset," she said. Sam's hair was like straw, and it stuck out all over her head. She shuddered in her sleep.

I reached over and smoothed a strand away from her face. "I'm going to find out who did this to her."

Daisy took Sam's hand and murmured, "Here goes nothing." And that's the last thing she said for several minutes.

I was afraid to look away.

Samantha's prone form began to thrash, and Daisy's grip tightened.

I watched; every muscle in my body tensed. Then Samantha's body stopped moving and went still, her mouth open in a soundless scream.

Daisy let out a high-pitched wail. I yanked on her arm, but she didn't let go of Sam's hand. I tried again, and Daisy finally broke free and then collapsed on the floor, gasping.

I helped Daisy to her feet. Her blue eyes were wide and she was shaking.

"Are you okay?" I asked. "Here, sit down and have a drink of water."

After she had a few minutes to recover, I asked, "Did you find anything out?"

"Screaming," she said. "Over and over. All I heard was the sound of Samantha screaming."

"Did you notice anything else?"

"Give me a minute," she said. She started to shake again.

I grabbed an extra blanket at the foot of the bed and draped it over her.

"Thanks," she said. "Jessica, there was someone else there with us. Someone Sam was deathly afraid of."

"Did you get a good look?"

She shook her head. "It was just a shadowy figure. It was big, though."

"Did you see anything else?"

"No," she said.

"Do you feel up to trying again in a few days?"

She nodded. "In the meantime, we should try to find out where Sam went, who she talked to right before this happened."

Sean came into the room as we were leaving, holding a teddy bear that said "Get Well Soon." "Any change?"

He didn't seem to notice Daisy at first. I nudged him. "Daisy was trying to make contact with Sam psychically," I explained.

"Hi, Daisy," he said, finally noticing his friend.

She gave him a hug.

"She's still not conscious," Sean said. "What are we going to do?"

"We're working on it," Daisy said. "Jessica and I are going to find out what happened to her, I promise."

He sat next to Samantha and picked up her hand. "I hope so."

"We need to find out what she was doing before she fell into this trance, or whatever it is," I said. "I know you two talked or texted every day. Was anything out of the ordinary going on with her?"

"It's the beginning of the quarter," he said. "She has new classes."

"What kind of classes?" I asked.

"The usual. She did mention an art class, though."

"Do you know the name of the professor?"

There was a long pause while he thought about it. "He's young, for a professor, and really into surrealism. At least that's what Sam said."

I was still processing the fact that my brother knew what surrealism was.

"I remember something else," he said. "Sam was at a stable but she wasn't riding horses. She had some field trip for botany class."

"I'll go check it out," I told him.

"Jess, thanks," he said. "But take someone with you. And be careful."

"I will," I assured him.

I'd have to wait for the right opportunity. Mr. Platsky didn't seem like he'd give us an open invitation to snoop around his farm anytime soon.

"Try to get some rest," Daisy said. But Sean wasn't listening. He clung tight to his girlfriend's hand and begged her to come back to him.

Daisy and I left the hospital but my thoughts stayed there. Was Samantha the victim of a Mara? Or was there something else sinister going on in Nightshade?

CHAPTER NINE

Since her Vegas elopement, Flo had mellowed out a bit about the nonstop training. But now that there had been a few murders in Nightshade, she expected us to patrol.

The doctor, and more importantly, Mom, decided my ankle had healed enough that I could return to moderate exercise — which meant that my Saturday night was going to involve a hot date patrolling the streets with my fellow viragoes instead of a hot date with my boyfriend.

Andy picked me up and we headed for Main Street. She parked in front of Slim's. The other v-girls were already there, but there was a surprise visitor.

"Dominic's mom is joining us on patrol?" I asked, dismayed.

"I know," Andy said. "Isn't it great?"

"Yeah, great."

We got out of the car and joined them.

I took the opportunity to catch everyone up on the

latest news. "Samantha Devereaux is in a coma," I explained. "And I think it has something to do with the nightmare murders."

"Who do you think is behind it?" Flo asked.

I shrugged.

"Spit it out," Andy demanded. "We don't have all day."

"Andy!" Raven said.

"No, she's right," I said. "I don't know. I don't know how long Samantha can hold on. We need to figure something out."

"We'll help however we can," Raven said softly.

"Thanks, Raven," I said. I hugged her.

"Jessica, Mom's going to lead the patrol tonight," Raven said.

I looked at Flo. "Is that true?" As our virago leader, she'd never given up control before. She loved bossing us around.

"You follow Lydia's orders," Flo confirmed. "No questions."

I had questions. Major questions, but I knew Flo would give me her death stare if I dared to open my mouth. So I didn't.

"We'll break into teams," Mrs. Gray said. "Raven, you go with Andy. Jessica, you're with me."

"With you? What about Flo?" I dreaded the idea of spending time alone with Dominic's mom, and Raven looked disappointed that her mother hadn't partnered with her.

"Flo's staying here," Mrs. Gray said. "Any more questions? Or can we get started?"

"We can get started," I said.

We divided the town into four quadrants and then went our separate ways. Mrs. Gray didn't say anything until we reached the park.

"How's your ankle?" she asked.

"The doctor gave me the all-clear." I was touched by her concern, but the feeling was short-lived.

"Then stop babying it and get a move on," she snapped.

"Yes, Mrs. Gray," I replied.

"Call me Lydia. We'll be spending a lot of time together."

"We will?" I asked, but her attention was drawn to something on the path up ahead of us.

"Did you see that?"

"What?"

Mrs. Gray had already sprinted ahead.

I followed her but she was fast. I saw a flash of white as she ran through a copse of trees.

I caught up to her in the middle of the park. She was watching a ghostly white horse drinking water from the fountain.

"It's here again," I whispered.

Raven's mom put a finger to her lips. We watched the horse in silence until its ears went back, as if it heard something. The horse galloped off, but this time Mrs. Gray didn't chase after it.

"You've seen this horse before?" she asked.

"On the beach, right before school started."

"And you didn't bother to tell anyone that a Mara was in town?" She made her contempt for me obvious.

"I didn't know it was a Mara then, but I did tell Flo what we'd seen."

"We?"

"It was the night Tashya came to town," I said. "Everyone at the bonfire saw it."

"Tashya's not the Mara," Mrs. Gray said sharply.

"I never said she was," I responded. "Especially since I don't even know that much about what a Mara is."

"You will," she said. "You will." But she didn't bother to provide any further information. I resolved I'd find out more on my own.

On Sunday, we took a break from our virago duties. Everyone had been invited to the Black Opal to watch Side Effects May Vary's practice.

The Black Opal was an all-ages club. The interior

was painted in vivid colors and the ceiling was sky blue with fluffy white clouds. A bright orange portrait of Teddie Myles, the owner and legendary rock goddess, was displayed prominently on the wall behind the stage.

"Any news on Samantha?" Flo asked.

"None," I said. "Daisy is going to try again to reach her telepathically, but she needs all the help we can give her. Any ideas?"

"Maybe changing what she's dreaming about will wake her from her coma," Raven said.

I stared at her. "That's genius."

"Could we knock the shadowy figure out of her dream somehow?" Andy asked.

"Maybe Daisy and Rose could help us with that," I said.

"I wonder how Sam has survived when the others didn't," Raven said.

"Sam is tough," I replied. "And she's best friends with Daisy. The two of them have seen plenty of strange things before this."

"Or maybe she wasn't the intended victim?" Flo said as she took a doughnut from her bag and chewed it contemplatively.

"You told us no desserts during training, Flo," Andy pointed out.

"And you thought I was serious?" she said.

Bert, the manager of Side Effects May Vary, approached our table with the band in tow and handed everyone Cranky Kitten T-shirts.

"What's the occasion?" I asked.

"Did you tell them the tour was moved up?" Flo's husband, Vinnie, asked.

Dominic gave me a nervous look. "I was just about to."

"We've got a couple of months to prepare," Vinnie said. "And then we're hitting the road."

I turned to Dominic. "What about school?" I asked. "I thought you weren't going until after graduation."

He shrugged. "Most of the tour is during winter break. And Aunt Katrina is going to tutor me on the road the rest of the time. The school's already agreed."

"Sounds like everything's all settled," I said.

"Jessica, don't be like that," Dominic said.

"When were you going to tell me?" I asked in a low voice, but I could feel his band mates' eyes on me. I was being the difficult girlfriend. I wanted to be happy for them, but I was too angry.

"I was going to tell you," Dominic said. "But I knew you would be upset."

"You were right."

"How long are you going to be gone?" I braced myself.

"A month. All of December." He said it quickly.

"You'll be gone during Christmas? And New Year's Eve?"

He nodded miserably.

"I thought we'd have your senior year together at least."

"We will have most of it," he assured me. "I'll be around for Homecoming and prom."

Most? He looked so distressed that I felt like a horrible girlfriend.

I sighed. "I guess it won't be so bad. We can still talk every day."

He brightened. "I can send you videos."

He got to his feet as the rest of the band started to tune up.

"I've got to go," Dominic said awkwardly. "But we'll talk more about it later, okay?"

"Okay."

He kissed the top of my head. "I'll be back before you even miss me."

That was highly doubtful.

My anger disappeared as quickly as it had arrived. I had bigger things to worry about. Like catching a killer.

He joined the rest of the band onstage, and Vinnie on drums led off the set. Dominic stepped up to the mike and started to strum the new song, but then a strange look crossed his face. He was about to provide a clue — at least I hoped he would.

"'Runnin' Down a Dream.'" Flo identified the song for us. "Tom Petty."

"Why can't the killer's name just be in the song title for once?" I grumbled, jokingly.

"Let's take a break," Vinnie said quickly after Dominic was done singing the song. Most of the band had accepted Dominic's being a seer, but Jeff Cool, the guitarist, was frowning. He was less than cool about Dominic's predictions throwing off their set list.

Jeff stomped outside. The break was really a time-out for him. Everyone in the band was sick of his whiny prima donna behavior. I wondered how they were going to survive a month on a tour bus with him.

Dominic and his aunt Katrina went to Teddie's office, I assumed to go over the band's schedule with her. Or maybe just to say hi. Everyone liked Teddie.

Flo, Raven, Andy, and I sat at the table discussing the latest development. "Why do my brother's clues have to be so cryptic?" Raven complained.

Maybe they weren't cryptic at all. "Runnin' Down a Dream." Eva had told me she was having nightmares and had been dreaming of someone or something running. It sounded sort of like what had happened to Sam, and I didn't want Eva to end up like that. I told the other v-girls what was happening to my best friend.

"We've got to spend the night at Eva's," I said urgently.

CHAPTER TEN

I called Eva to make sure it was okay that we stay over, and after rehearsal, Andy, Raven, and I headed to her house.

The Harris house was spotless and decorated in soothing beige, blue, and white, except for Eva's room, which was lime green and purple and far from spotless. She loved to collect items for the horror movie she planned to make one day. A life-size cardboard cutout of Vincent Price stood in one corner, and her pet raven Poe's cage in another.

We ordered pizza and played board games late into the night.

"So what's the plan?" Eva asked. "I have a Spanish test tomorrow and I haven't had much sleep in days."

"You can go to sleep and we'll watch you," I said. If a Mara was haunting the dreams of my best friend, I was going to catch it.

We laid out our sleeping bags as Poe watched us from his perch.

"No wonder you can't sleep with that thing in here," Andy said.

"Poe's not a thing!" Eva said indignantly. "He's a smart boy. Aren't you?" she cooed to her pet.

"Nevermore!" he croaked. She beamed like a proud mama and gave him a cracker.

Raven opened her bag and took out her laptop. "I'm going to try a little research," she said. "Otherwise, what are we going to do if Eva does get a visit from the night mare?"

"Good idea," I said.

"Here we go," Raven said, after a few minutes of searching. "There's something called a night hag. Red glowing eyes, screechy voice. Some of the legends say that if you call a night hag by name, she'll leave you alone."

"That's helpful, if we actually knew who it was," Andy said sarcastically.

Raven frowned.

"The information is still useful," I told Andy. "Anything else, Raven?"

"If you put something metal under your bed, it will keep the nightmares away," she said.

"We should try it," I suggested. "It can't hurt."

Eva went to the kitchen and came back with a couple of forks. "Will this work?"

Raven laughed. "As long as you put it under your bed and not under your mattress, it might do the trick."

After a while, the rhythmic tapping of Raven's keyboard was putting me into a sleep-deprived trance. I was trying not to doze off, but failing.

"We should have picked up some coffee at Slim's," I said, smothering a yawn.

Andy held up a thermos. "Do you want it plain or with sugar?"

"Sugar, please," I said. "And milk."

"There's some in the fridge," Eva said. "Help yourself. In fact, I'll go with you. Let's pop some popcorn."

"You sure it's a good idea to eat right before bedtime?" I asked.

"Why not?" she asked.

"My mom says sleeping on a full stomach can give you bad dreams," I said.

"Not to mention indigestion," she said. "But it's just popcorn."

Eva put a packet of popcorn in the microwave, and the buttery smell made my stomach growl.

Eva's sister, Bethany, came into the kitchen. From the way she was dressed, it was pretty clear she'd just come home from a date.

"You're out past your curfew," Eva commented. "Mom's gonna kill you."

"Mom won't know," Bethany replied.

Eva crossed her arms over her chest. "Not unless I tell her."

"Don't forget, I have dirt on you, too," Bethany countered.

"What kind of dirt?" I asked.

"Nothing," Eva said quickly. "Bethany's just trying to scare me. Right, Bethany?"

"Right," Bethany agreed, but she wouldn't look at me. "I'm going to bed."

"Good-night," we called after her.

"What was all that about?" I asked, after I was sure Bethany was out of earshot.

"Nothing."

"It didn't sound like nothing."

"It's just sister stuff," Eva said. She changed the subject. "Thanks for staying with me."

"Are you kidding me? I'm worried about you. I didn't even know you could *get* scared." Eva's penchant for horror movies made her extremely hard to spook.

She laughed, but it was a halfhearted effort.

I grabbed mugs and milk and sugar for the coffee and Eva took the popcorn. I followed her back to her room.

Everyone else was sleeping, even Andy, who'd boasted that she'd be able to outlast everyone.

I held the thermos of coffee and poured myself a cup, then added milk and a generous helping of sugar.

I wandered over to Eva's desk, where a wooden figure sprawled across her desk blotter. "Is this your art project? Who is it going to be?"

"Hey, no peeking," she said. She threw a sweater over the marionette.

"You can't tell me? Not even a hint?" I tried to wheedle it out of her, but she wouldn't spill.

"I want it to be a surprise," she said. "But I think you're going to like it."

Eva settled into her bed with Ted Vicious, her punk rocker teddy bear.

"Remember, if anything happens," I said, "try to imagine something else. Something that makes you happy."

"Did you seriously just tell me to go to my happy place?" she asked. "The only thing that would make me happy right now is sleep."

"Go ahead," I said. "I'll stay up and keep watch."

"I'll try," she said. She plumped up her pillow and in seconds was out.

Moonlight shone through the window and I went to pull down the shade.

I looked down and saw a shadowy figure standing in the yard. The person seemed to be looking up at me, but instead of a face, there was only blackness.

I stepped back. My heart was beating so loud that it seemed it would wake my sleeping friends. When I looked again, the shadowy figure was gone.

Then there was a thump above me. Like something heavy had landed on the roof. Poe started squawking, but I shushed him with a cracker.

The noise came again. It sounded like someone was walking on the roof. "It's probably just a squirrel or a bird or something," I said to myself.

"That's a pretty big bird," Raven said.

"I thought you were sleeping."

"I was," she yawned. "But that thumping woke me up."

The noise stopped as suddenly as it had begun.

I crossed to the window and looked down. A clown stood under the streetlight. There was blood dripping from its mouth. I screamed.

The sound woke up the other girls and brought Eva's mom dashing into the room. "What's going on?"

I couldn't tell the truth. Mrs. Harris would think I was crazy.

I moved away from the window. "Sorry, I had a bad dream. I didn't mean to scream."

"Did you girls watch *Dawn of the Dead* before bed?" she scolded. "I told Eva that would lead to nightmares."

"No," I said. "But I had one of those dreams where I showed up to school without any clothes on."

"I've had those dreams before," Raven said.

Eva's mom seemed to believe my excuse. "Well, go back to bed, girls. You have school in the morning."

After she left the room a groggy Eva said, "What really happened?"

"I saw a freaky clown with blood dripping down its face." I hated clowns more than anything. "Clowns scare me."

"Me, too," Eva admitted.

Raven ticked away on her laptop. "Actually, fear of clowns is a phobia."

"What's it called?"

"Being human," Andy said dryly.

"It's called coulrophobia," Raven said. "But Andy's right. A lot of people are afraid of clowns."

"Eva, did you dream while you were sleeping?"

She shook her head. "That was the most sleep I've had all week."

"Speaking of which," Andy said, "We have to be at school in five hours. I suggest we all try to get some shut-eye."

Eva yawned. "Sounds good to me." Within seconds, she was out cold. The other viragoes dropped off, but I couldn't sleep. The vision of the creepy clown smirking up at me stayed with me the rest of the night. I finally dozed off at dawn.

Andy drove us to school the next morning. I was too tired to bother with my hair, so it stood out wildly. Raven and I sat in the back seat and Eva rode shotgun.

"Nice hair," Andy said. Her blond curls weren't much better.

I grabbed a rubber band and quickly braided my hair into one long plait. "There. Better?"

"Much," Raven said. "Now do mine."

"Eva, do you want me to do your hair when we get to school?"

She was staring out the window, in a fog. "Eva?" I repeated.

"Can we stop for coffee and doughnuts?" she finally said. "I think some sugar and grease will do me good."

"We can make a quick stop at the Donut Hole," Andy said. "But we have to hurry. I don't want another tardy."

The doughnut shop was busy and Andy had a hard time finding parking. She circled the block once and we got lucky when Raven spotted an open space. Andy turned on her blinker to pull in, but a flashy black sports car cut her off and nabbed the spot. A guy with dark shades and an attitude got out of the car.

"What a jerk!" Andy said.

"That's Mr. Martin," Eva said. "Maybe he just didn't see us."

"Yeah, right," Andy snorted.

We pulled into a spot two spaces down and entered the crowded shop. Andy kept checking her watch until it was time for us to order.

"How can an art teacher afford a car like that?" Raven whispered.

Eva shrugged. "The marionettes he makes sell for a lot of money."

"They would have to be pretty expensive to afford that car," I said. "It's at least a hundred thousand dollars."

"How do you know?" Eva asked.

"It's Sean's dream car," I said. "He has posters in his room and everything."

We grabbed our doughnuts and left. We almost bumped into Mr. Martin outside, but he ignored us and hopped back into his car. He gunned the motor and took off with a squeal of the tires.

"What a jerk!" Andy said again.

This time, even Eva didn't argue with her.

CHAPTER ELEVEN

We weren't the only kids at school who looked like they'd been missing out on sleep. Several of my classmates carried giant cups of coffee or energy drinks. A couple of kids were still wearing pajama bottoms, and I saw my sister Sarah in the hallway wearing her fuzzy slippers.

The entire day consisted of people bumping into each other. There was almost a fire in the cafeteria when one of the lunch ladies fell asleep with the world's largest lasagna in the oven. Fortunately, Principal Amador smelled something burning and caught it in time.

During lunch, the other viragoes and I interviewed as many kids as possible, but they all said the same thing. They didn't remember anything but the sound of running and then they woke up screaming.

But I got a different answer when I asked my sister Sarah about it. "Did you have a nightmare?"

"I saw a white horse," she said. "Red eyes, steam coming from its nose. Weird, huh?"

"Not as weird as you'd think," I said. She'd always been able to describe her dreams in detail.

Selena Silvertongue came up to me right after the bell rang. "Jessica, I know you can handle this on your own, but I thought I should tell you something."

I braced myself. "Go ahead."

"I've been hearing rumors about the murders," she said. "And I think the killer might be using black magic."

Selena was not only an up-and-coming witch herself, but she was also the niece of a powerful sorceress, so I took her hunch very seriously. "What makes you say that?"

"I'm not an expert, but it's possible to murder someone without even being in the room using black magic."

"What does your aunt say?" Circe Silvertongue was not a particularly nice person, but she knew her magic.

"She's out of town," Selena said. "She's in Europe with the count. Liam and his sister Claudia are keeping an eye on me." Liam Dracul was Poppy Giordano's boyfriend and a vampire, which made him a pretty good temporary guardian.

"Thanks, Selena," I said. "It's a good lead. If you think of anything else, let me know."

After lunch, Noel Sebastian got yelled at in Biology when he fell asleep and started to snore. By sixth period, Jimmy Garfinkle was doing a brisk business in black market soda.

Eva and I walked home together. "I'm so glad today was an early dismissal day," she said. She smothered a yawn. There was almost an accident at the corner when a driver nearly ran a red light. Tires screeched as another car tried to stop and narrowly avoided a collision.

"Jeesh," Eva said. "I think everyone could use a little sleep."

"You're telling me," I said. "We better figure out who or what is causing this before someone else gets hurt."

When I got home, Daisy's car was in her driveway, so I headed to her house. I wanted to see if she'd picked up anything, psychically speaking.

"How was school?" she asked.

"Dangerous," I said. I told her about all the near misses.

"Half the town is walking around like zombies," Daisy said.

"Been there, done that," I replied. "Who could be behind this?"

Daisy's eyes narrowed. "Let's make some brownies. Baking always helps me think."

"So this is the secret to Ryan's heart?" I asked as she got out the ingredients. "Brownies?"

She laughed. "Not just any brownies. Caramel brownies made from scratch."

"Sounds like anybody would love them."

She grinned. "We'll make a double batch. One for Ryan and one for Dominic."

"I'm not very handy in the kitchen," I warned her.

"You don't have to be," she assured me. "This is the easiest recipe in the world."

She handed me a spatula.

"What's it like being a psychic?"

"What's it like being a virago?" she countered.

"Harder than it sounds," we said at once.

We looked at each other and burst out laughing.

"So Dominic is pretty cute," Daisy said.

"And so is Ryan," I replied.

"I used to be nervous about that when we first started dating," she admitted.

"You? But you're gorgeous!"

She got out the butter, cream, and sugar. "Have you seen my sisters? Or my mom? They're truly gorgeous," she said. "But I've learned that it's what's inside that matters."

I was still struggling with the idea that Daisy Giordano didn't realize how pretty she was. She had electric blue eyes and creamy skin, which, paired with her dark hair, were stunning. But her kindness was probably the most beautiful thing about her.

We whipped up a double batch of brownies, and Daisy slid them into the oven.

"But you have to deal with the whole lead singer thing," Daisy commented.

"You mean the fans," I grumbled. "You can say it."

"Dominic looks at you like you're the only girl in the room," Daisy said. "So I wouldn't worry about it."

"His ex-girlfriend's in town," I said. "And his mother hates me."

"His mother doesn't like you?" Daisy asked. "Isn't she a virago too?"

I nodded. "I wouldn't be surprised to find out that she invited Dominic's ex here just to try to break us up."

"That's horrible," Daisy said. "Ryan's dad was great. I miss him."

"Everyone in Nightshade misses Chief Mendez." Ryan's dad, the former chief of police, had been killed on his son's grad night.

There was a melancholy silence before the oven timer went off.

"Did they catch everyone in the Scourge?" I asked.

The Scourge was the nefarious agency behind the grad night bomb and the deaths of other paranormal residents of Nightshade. "I know Sam's dad was the leader, but it's over now that he's in jail, right?"

She shrugged. "I don't think it will ever be over as long as people hate other people."

My phone alerted me to a new text from Dominic.

"Hey, want to go watch Side Effects May Vary record their first album?" I asked.

"Sounds interesting," Daisy said. "But where?"

"Teddie Myles has a recording studio at her house," I said. "And we're invited."

CHAPTER TWELVE

Teddie Myles lived on an estate on a hill near the Wilder property. The house was more modern looking than the Wilders', and I could see an enormous guitar-shaped pool through the trees. Before she opened the Black Opal, Teddie had been a successful musician, but I'd never realized that she was so rich.

Daisy parked in the long driveway right next to a newer-model BMW. The slick luxury car didn't really seem like Teddie's style. The old dusty Jeep, its tailgate nearly covered with bumper stickers, seemed more her speed.

Jensen Kenton got out of the BMW.

"Hi, Mr. Kenton," I said. "What are you doing here?"

He didn't seem to mind my nosy question. "Ms. Myles just bought one of my new paintings. I wanted to deliver it personally."

He pulled the painting from the car and held it out to inspect it. "Would you mind shutting the trunk for me?"

As I did so, I noticed an open container of miscellaneous stuff that looked like a lost and found box.

"Why are you girls here today?" Mr. Kenton asked as we walked to the house.

"My boyfriend's band is recording here," I explained. "They won the Battle of the Bands a few months ago and the prize was a recording contract with Cranky Kitten Records."

"Sounds interesting."

"Interesting is one way of describing it." I was pretty sure we'd run into Talulah Crank, the owner of Cranky Kitten Records. Cranky also described her personality.

I rang the doorbell, since Mr. Kenton's arms were full.

Dominic must have been waiting for us because he opened the door on the first ring.

Jensen Kenton didn't bother to say hello, just shouldered his way past Dominic and kept going with the painting through an arched doorway.

"Thanks for coming," Dominic said to me and Daisy.

"I've never been to a recording session before," Daisy said.

"Me, neither," Dominic said with a smile.

"Are we late?" I asked.

"No, perfect timing. I'm happy you're here," he said. "Don't freak out, okay?"

"About what?"

"Mom's here too," he said. "And she brought Tashya."

He gave me a quick kiss. "The recording studio is on the top floor. I'll meet you there. I've got to warm up before they record the vocals."

As he left, Daisy and I exchanged a look. "Don't worry. You brought a secret weapon, remember?" she said, holding up the Tupperware container full of brownies.

We followed the sound of voices into the living room. Teddie was holding court at a baby grand piano. Her hair was striped green today and she had on a CBGB tee and black leather pants and purple Converse sneakers.

"Daisy, Jessica," she said. "Glad you could make it."

"Thanks for letting us observe," I said.

Talulah Crank stood. "I managed to pull a few strings," she said smugly. Talulah was tall, with short, choppy black hair and frosty green eyes.

Teddie let out a bark of laughter. "Let me show you where the recording studio is," she said, ignoring Talulah's posturing.

"Are you singing with the band?" Teddie asked as she led us upstairs.

"I don't think so," I said. "I'm pretty sure they don't want their lead singer's girlfriend horning in."

"You and Dominic sound good together. You guys

should try another duet." Dominic and I had sung a duet at the Battle of the Bands in the spring, but we still hadn't settled on a new song for the choir audition.

Daisy and I followed Teddie to the third floor. We walked along a hallway with white carpeting and white walls. The starkness was alleviated by huge framed photos of Teddie during her glory days. One photo had her sitting on the lap of an extremely handsome well-known rocker. I stopped to take a closer look.

"My first love," Teddie sighed.

The next photo showed her playing guitar in an all-female powerhouse rock band.

"Is this where you're going to hang your new painting?" I asked when we reached an expanse of blank wall.

She looked startled. "How did you know about that?"

"We met Jensen Kenton on the way in," Daisy explained. "He had your painting with him."

"I wonder where he got off to," Teddie said, but she didn't seem too concerned.

"Is it one of his scary pieces?" I asked.

"No," she said. "I don't really care for his work. I bought one of his older, tamer landscape pieces for Lola." Teddie's sister, Lola Wells, was chief of police in Nightshade, which was kind of mind-boggling. They seemed so different.

"This is my favorite room in the house," Teddie said,

throwing open the door to the recording studio. "Go on, girls, take a look."

"Can't you see we're busy recording?" Tashya snapped before she realized it was Teddie standing behind Daisy and me.

"You're not recording," Teddie replied calmly. "Or the light above the door would have been lit up like a Christmas tree."

Tashya looked sulky and crossed her arms.

On the opposite wall was a state-of-the-art soundboard manned by an older guy with a fedora perched on his head.

"This is my buddy Josh," Teddie said. "Best engineer in the business."

"This place is amazing," I said.

Tashya snorted, but subsided when Daisy gave her a warning look.

"This is the control room," Teddie explained. Above the soundboard a window looked into another room with microphones all over the place. "And that is where the band will be recording."

Right now, Dominic and his mom were the only ones on the other side of the glass. They appeared to be having a heated conversation.

Teddie's cell rang and she stepped out of the studio, saying, "Excuse me, I've got to take this."

"I wonder what those two are talking about," I muttered before I could stop myself.

Josh the engineer shrugged. "Easy to find out," he said, and pressed a button on the soundboard that allowed us to hear what was going on in the recording room.

I heard Dominic's raised voice. "Why did you invite her here, Mom?"

"Truthfully?" she replied.

"It'd be a nice change."

"Because I wanted the two of you to get back together," she said.

Dominic's mom really did not like me one bit. I knew I shouldn't eavesdrop, but I couldn't help myself. I was dying to know why his mom was playing matchmaker.

"That's never going to happen," Dominic said. "I'm dating Jessica."

"But Tashya's devoted to you and she's not . . ."

"Not what?"

"Not a virago," she said.

That's why Dom's mom hated me so much? It was the last thing I expected.

I cleared my throat, loudly, and Josh quickly yanked his hand from the button, muting the conversation between Dominic and Mrs. Gray. Tashya gave me a wicked smile, her eyes gleaming.

A few seconds later, Dominic and his mom entered

the control room. "There you are," he said to me. "I was wondering where you were."

"Hello, Jessica," Mrs. Gray said. "I thought you'd want to spend your time training instead of running after my son."

"I like spending time with him," I said. "And I train as much as any other virago."

I wanted to get away from Mrs. Gray and Tashya, so I asked Dom, "Do you want to work on our duet before the band gets here?"

"We're trying to narrow down our choices for our choir audition," Dominic explained to his mom.

"I didn't know Jessica was in chorus with you," she said.

"We've performed together lots of times," he said. "Which you'd know if you'd been around."

I felt awkward witnessing their squabbling, so I stepped into the vocal booth and turned on the mike. I cleared my throat and then launched into "Sally's Song" from *The Nightmare Before Christmas*. The mournful tune suited my mood perfectly.

When the last notes died away and I looked through the glass to the control room, I was surprised to see Mrs. Gray break into loud applause. "Jessica, I had no idea you were so talented," I heard her say. Tashya was scowling.

"I'm not just a virago," I said pointedly.

94

Dominic gave his mom a dirty look. I guess he figured out I'd overheard their conversation.

"What do you think of that song for our audition?" I asked him when I returned to the control room.

"I like it," Dominic replied.

Vinnie and Flo arrived, holding hands. Her T-shirt was a less snarky than her usual ones. It read I'M NOT YOUR HONEY, GIRL, OR SWEETHEART.

"Jessica, I didn't know you were going to be here today," Flo said. "Good. I need to talk to you. Daisy, you can come too."

Flo took us out into the hallway and said, "There's been another murder."

"Another one?"

"Marlon Sanguine," Flo said. "He was an older vampire. Didn't even have his fangs anymore. Completely harmless. Count Dracul already heard and is flipping out long-distance."

"Why would anyone want to hurt him? Are you sure he was harmless?"

"Completely," Flo said. "Have you and Daisy made any progress?"

I hadn't mentioned that Daisy and I were working together, but I'd learned long ago that Flo knew everything.

"I'm having a hard time tuning in to people's

thoughts," Daisy admitted. "Everyone in town is missing out on their sleep, which means they're not guarding their thoughts as much as usual."

"So you're getting too much information instead of not enough."

"Yep, it's like everyone is talking at once."

"I have suspicions about Jensen Kenton's paintings being behind it," I piped up.

"Did you see any paintings that might frighten a vampire?" Flo asked.

"You mean with garlic or wooden stakes or anything? No."

"Maybe it was the Mara," she said.

"I thought Maras only came out at night," I replied. "And wouldn't a vampire sleep during the day?"

"That's true," Flo said, looking troubled.

I brought up my other theory. "What if someone has found a way to use a painting to haunt people's dreams?"

"Jessica, you may be on to something," Flo said. "I'll ask Raven to research it."

Raven was the pacifist in our little group, which was weird for a warrior. But Flo seemed to understand that Raven was more comfortable looking things up than kicking butt.

"We should try to find out who bought paintings from the exhibit," I suggested.

When the rest of Side Effects May Vary arrived, we focused on music instead of murder for a few hours.

Dominic's mom was sitting next to Tashya on a long couch against one wall of the control room. I walked to the other end of the room and pretended to study the framed concert posters on the wall.

At one point while Dominic was recording vocals, there seemed to be a problem. Josh said, "Try it again" into the microphone before he handed Teddie a headset.

Dominic tried again, but I could tell something was wrong. Then his eyes rolled back and I knew what was going on.

I tapped Teddie on the shoulder. "Can you tell what he's singing?"

She listened for a moment. "It's a song called 'Black Heart,'" she replied. "Does that mean anything to you?"

It meant something. I just didn't know what. The rest of the recording session went smoothly, but on the way home, I turned the clue over and over in my mind.

CHAPTER THIRTEEN

After the visit to the studio, we went to Dominic's house to watch a movie and finally enjoy the brownies I had made. We had the house to ourselves, since Raven, his mom, and his aunt were at dinner in San Carlos.

"Jensen Kenton is helping with the decorations at the Wilder estate for the Day of the Dead party," Dominic said after polishing off his third brownie. I guessed I was a better baker than I had thought.

"He doesn't really seem like the community service type," I observed.

"I did hear something interesting the other day," Dominic said. "About Mr. Martin. Did you know he was related to Mrs. Lincoln?"

"He was?"

He nodded. "He was her nephew. I heard it from Mrs. Wilder."

"Where did you see Mrs. Wilder?" The elderly matriarch of the shape-shifting Wilder family rarely left her estate these days.

"My mom and I went to dinner there," he said. There was something in his voice that made me uncomfortable.

"Special occasion?" I asked. Wilder's was a fancy eatery on the estate. I tried not to let it bother me that I hadn't been invited.

He took a deep breath. "It was for Tashya's birthday."

"Take me home," I said. "Now."

"Jess, it didn't mean anything."

I was furious. "I'm glad that something like going to dinner with your ex-girlfriend was so meaningless that you didn't even tell me about it."

"I'm telling you about it now," he said.

"Too late."

"Jessica, it was my mom's idea," he said. "I didn't even want to go."

"But you did. And I know your mom doesn't like us together," I snapped.

I thought he'd try to deny it, but he didn't.

"My mom doesn't run my life," he said.

"If that's true, then why did you go out with Tashya?"

"I didn't go out with Tashya."

"Close enough," I retorted.

"Why do you let her get to you?" he asked.

I crossed my arms. "Why do you?"

"Look, I didn't ask Tashya to come here," he said. "And she was my girlfriend when I was a sophomore. That was ages ago."

"How would you feel if my ex-boyfriend followed me around all day?" I asked.

"You mean like Connor does?"

"Connor? What are you talking about? He's dating Selena."

"He still has a thing for you," Dominic insisted. "And he's in half of your classes."

"You sound jealous," I said, but he had a point.

"Maybe I am."

"It never occurred to me that you might get jealous," I said. "You have girls hanging all over you all the time. Half of them would like to push me down the stairs just to get next to you. Including Tashya."

He pulled me into his arms. "What else can I do to prove to you that you're the only one for me?"

"Kiss me," I replied.

He leaned in seductively. "Have I convinced you?" His breath warmed my lips, but he was still too far away.

"Yes." I grabbed the back of his neck and pulled him closer.

We sprang apart when the front door opened. His family had returned home.

"Jessica, nice to see you," Mrs. Gray said. And she

actually sounded like she meant it. "We brought dessert. Would you like to join us?"

I glanced at the clock. "I'd love to, but it's almost my curfew. I'd better get home."

I smiled all the way back to my house. Mrs. Gray was finally warming up to me, which meant it wouldn't be long before Tashya figured out it was time to leave Nightshade.

But Tashya show no signs of departing when I got to school the next day. She and Harmony were standing about a foot from my locker. I was sure it was deliberate, and their loud conversation only confirmed my suspicions.

"Isn't it gorgeous?" Tashya held out her hand in a flamboyant way.

"He gave you a ring?" Harmony asked. "And such an expensive one."

"Yes, for my birthday," she boasted. "And he took me to Wilder's."

I gritted my teeth as Tashya and Harmony swanned away. I knew she was baiting me, but I couldn't help the jealousy I was feeling.

Raven overheard them and walked over to me. "Ignore them," she said. "Dom didn't give Tashya that ring."

"Are you sure?"

"Positive," Raven replied. "It came from her parents."

"Why is she trying to make it seem like it's from Dominic, then?"

"C'mon, Jessica," she said. "You know why. She wants Dominic back. But he's not buying it."

"I wish I were as sure of that as you are."

"Sure of what?" Dominic asked. I'd been so caught up watching Tashya that I hadn't noticed him approaching.

Raven opened her mouth to explain, but I shook my head at her.

"It's nothing," I said. "Tashya's just trying to make everyone think that you gave her a ring for her birthday."

"A ring?" Dominic repeated. "Why would I give her a ring?"

"And more importantly, why would she think I'd be stupid enough to believe it?" I scoffed. I didn't add that she was a good enough actor that she'd almost had me fooled.

He gave me a quick kiss. "Her dad gave her that ring. He was in town."

"I'm surprised her parents are letting her stay in Nightshade this long. Don't they miss her?"

He shrugged. "They travel a lot."

"Why is that?"

He hesitated. "Don't tell anyone, because Tashya is really sensitive about it, but her parents work for a traveling circus. The one that just rolled into town."

"A circus? She doesn't seem like the circus type at all."

I didn't want to say that Tashya seemed like she should be starring in *Mean Girls* or something. Still, learning that her family was in the circus made me wonder if she was somehow involved with the creepy clown I had seen outside Eva's house.

Harmony coincidentally brought Tashya to chorus practice that same day, when Dominic and I had our audition.

Or, judging from Tashya's smirk, maybe it wasn't a coincidence.

"Just ignore her," Dominic said. "You'll do great."

We were third in line. Connor and Selena did a skillful cover of Frank Sinatra's "Witchcraft," which I thought was pretty funny, considering that Selena is a sorceress. Connor's voice was strong, but had a little Tom Waits thing going for it. Raven and Eva sang a song from *A Nightmare on Elm Street.* Then it was our turn.

Dominic grabbed my hand as we headed to the microphones. I felt Tashya's eyes on me the whole time, and my voice started out shaky. But I finally hit my stride and the notes came out clear and strong. The song ended without any major goofs on my part. "Sally's Song" from *A Nightmare Before Christmas* seemed to be a hit, judging from the applause from the choir. Even Ms. Clare had a smile on her face.

CHAPTER FOURTEEN

On Wednesday it was back to Phantasm Farms. When Poppy honked the horn, I grabbed the gift bag containing Sanja's present and herded my sisters into the car.

It turned out that Mr. Platsky had rented out part of the farm to the circus, because when we arrived for our lesson, they were setting up the big top in the pasture near the main road.

"A circus!" Katie said. "Can we go?"

"Not today," I replied. "But once they're open, we'll go, I promise."

When we reached the stables, Poppy said, "I'll be a little late picking you up. I have to take Sydney and Sarah to the art supply store."

"How did we ever survive without you?" I asked her.

"I'm glad to do it," Poppy said. "College is expensive and your parents pay me well."

I had a good idea of what would be in store for me once I got my driver's license, and I was pretty sure I wouldn't be paid for it. Kind of made me rethink my eagerness to drive.

I waved goodbye to Poppy as Katie and Kellie raced ahead to the stable.

I stashed the gift bag under my jacket and purse and left them in the beat-up old locker Mr. Platsky had told us we could use for any valuables.

He had already saddled up our horses. I noticed that this time, I got a mild-mannered older mare instead of the horse who wanted to chomp me.

Mr. Platsky spent most of the time correcting the way I held the reins, but my two sisters seemed to be naturals. I didn't see any sign of Sanja during the ride.

Back at the barn we helped groom the horses, and then Mr. Platsky led them away for some oats and water. When I grabbed my stuff from the locker, Katie noticed the gift bag. "Who is that for?"

"A friend," I told her. "Let's wait by the picnic table."

"I'm hungry," Katie complained, so I fished a couple of graham crackers out of my backpack.

I caught a flash of white out of the corner of my eye and then Sanja appeared.

She looked as bedraggled as ever. I didn't understand it. There were plenty of dads, single or otherwise, who knew how to take care of their kids. My own dad braided hair like a pro and did most of the cooking. Mr. Platsky seemed to have no problem grooming horses, so surely he could manage to drag a comb through his daughter's hair once in a while.

"Hi, Sanja. These are my sisters Katie and Kellie," I said. "And this is for you." I held out the bag but she didn't take it.

"What is that?"

"It's a present," I said. "Just something little. Open it!"

She took it like it was a sack of poisonous snakes and looked at the brush and de-tangler inside with wonder.

"Sit down and I'll show you how to use it."

I made it through the worst of the tangles before Poppy pulled up. As soon as Sanja saw the car, she ran off. I was happy to see that she took the gifts with her.

My chance to snoop around Phantasm Farms came on Sunday when Mom casually mentioned that we wouldn't be having riding lessons after school that week.

"Mr. Platsky canceled," she said.

"Did he say why?"

"Something about needing to go out of town," Mom said. "Makeup session is Saturday."

I groaned inwardly. "I was going to go for a run on Saturday."

"Why don't you go after your lesson?" Mom suggested, but it was more of an order.

I couldn't get ahold of any of the other viragoes, so I called Dominic. "I need a favor," I said. "Want to go for a ride?"

"Alone with you? I'll pick you up in ten minutes."

I waited for him outside and opened the car door practically before he made it to a full stop.

"What's your hurry?" he asked. "You almost injured yourself getting into the car."

"Thanks for getting here so quickly," I said. "I wanted to get there before dark."

Dominic put the car into drive.

"Don't you want to know where we're going? You didn't even ask."

He smiled at me. "I don't care. I'm with you and that's all that matters."

"Even if we're going on a life-endangering recon mission?" I teased.

"Even then," he said. "Where to?"

I gave him directions to the horse farm. "Samantha went there for a plant-collecting trip before she went into a coma," I said. "Maybe the two events are connected somehow."

Dominic and I parked by the side of the road and hiked in. "Katie said she saw someone in the abandoned house," I told him as we walked along.

"What do you think the owner will do if we get caught?" he asked.

"Probably have us arrested for trespassing," I said. "But he's supposedly out of town. I wonder if he took his daughter, Sanja. She's like a feral child."

"You think you can help her?" Dominic asked.

I sighed. "I hope so."

As we approached the house, we heard raised voices. A young girl and a man were arguing.

"I think that's Sanja," I told Dominic.

"I didn't kill them!" Sanja cried. "I can't help it if I give them nightmares."

I couldn't hear the man's reply, but the slamming of the door was clear enough.

"Hide," I whispered. "Someone is coming."

Dominic and I crouched behind an overgrown shrub. Mr. Platsky stomped by us without a glance.

"He seems intense," Dominic said, once Mr. Platsky was out of earshot.

I nodded. "You're not kidding."

"Do you think we should look for Sanja?" Dominic asked. "Mr. Platsky was pretty angry."

I nodded. "Why would her own father leave her alone in that scary old house?"

We crept into the house, and several dark hallways later, we found Sanja by following the sound of her sobbing. She was in a room upstairs with the door closed.

"Sanja, it's me, Jessica Walsh," I said. I turned the knob but the door was locked.

"Don't open it!" she yelled. The fear in her voice startled me.

"Your dad isn't here," I said.

"I know," she replied softly. "Don't open the door. It's the only way."

"Why would your father lock you in here?" Dominic asked.

"It's the only way," Sanja said again.

"The only way for what?" I asked.

"The only way to make sure I don't kill anyone."

A shiver ran down my spine. "Why would you think you would kill anyone?"

The sound of sobbing came through the door again.

"Sanja, let us in, please?" I begged.

We waited a long time, but finally Sanja said, "There's a key hanging by the door."

I sighed with relief. There was indeed an old skeleton key on a hook by the door. I put it in the keyhole with shaky hands and turned the doorknob.

The rest of the house had been a living nightmare, but Sanja's room was warm and inviting. The walls were painted pale lavender, and a cheery quilt covered the bed.

"Tell us what's going on," Dominic said.

Sanja was trembling so hard she could hardly talk. "I'm a Mara," she finally said. I draped a blanket over her.

"What does that mean?" I asked. I knew that a Mara was a night mare who haunts sleeping victims, but I wanted her to keep talking.

"We transform into horses and scare people in their sleep. Sometimes the sound of our hooves is enough to terrify someone to death."

"You were the ghostly white horse we saw on the beach," I guessed.

"Yes," she confessed. "That was me."

"That must be why I sang 'Wild Horses' that night," Dom said.

Sanja hung her head, ashamed. "Father says that Maras are killers, that he locks me up for my own good," she said. "He left me a cell phone, just in case."

"Look, Sanja," I said. "I've been doing some research. We don't know for sure that a Mara is to blame for the deaths in Nightshade."

Dominic gave me a warning look, but I ignored it. I refused to believe that a little girl could be responsible for murder.

"Maybe not," she said. "But I killed my mother. Father tells me all the time."

"Maybe you misunderstood," Dominic said gently.

She shook her head. "My mother died when I was born. It's my fault she's gone. I'm a monster."

I gasped. What a horrible thing to tell a child. "Your father is the monster," I replied.

"Jessica, can I talk to you for a minute?" Dominic asked.

I followed him out into the dark hallway. "We should be careful," he warned. "We don't know what the truth is. Maybe her dad has a reason for what he's doing."

"For locking up his daughter?" I asked incredulously. "Sounds like superstition to me."

"I'm not championing his behavior," Dominic said. "But we need to be careful."

"I don't want to leave her here all alone."

"Me, neither. But what happens if it's true and we let her out?"

"It's not true," I insisted. "There's no way that innocent girl is a killer."

"Maybe not," he replied. "But we have to look at all the possibilities. She might not be the murderer, but we need to prove it."

"What should we do in the meantime? We can't just leave her there."

"She's safe and warm here," he said. "And what other choice do we have? What if we let her out and someone else dies?"

"Maybe she'll come stay with me," I suggested. We went back to Sanja's room and I posed the question, but she wouldn't budge.

"I'm better off here," Sanja said. "That way if someone dies tonight, at least I'll know it wasn't me."

"She has a point," Dominic said.

"Okay," I said. "We'll leave you alone. This time. But I'm coming over tomorrow to check on you."

She nodded. "That is acceptable."

I wrote down my cell phone number on a scrap of paper and handed it to her. "Call me if you need anything."

I knew we were doing the right thing, but it still broke my heart to leave Sanja and see her waving forlornly at us from her bedroom window.

After leaving the house, Dominic and I poked around the property looking for clues to Samantha's predicament, but we didn't find any unusual plants that might have put her in a coma. We left feeling down.

Despite Sanja's self-imprisonment, there was another dead body discovered the next day.

That's when I knew for sure she wasn't the killer.

CHAPTER **FIFTEEN**

On Monday, the rumor was buzzing around Nightshade High even before Principal Amador made the official announcement. The murder victim was Mr. Bellows, the shop teacher. "At least we know that Sanja didn't do it," I told Dominic.

"Do you think she got out somehow?" he asked me in a low voice.

I shook my head. "No way. Sanja was too scared to leave that room before sunrise, which means it's not a Mara."

"Then who is it?"

"Good question," I said. "Maybe it's time to follow up on the paintings. We know that at least two of the victims came into contact with Jensen Kenton's paintings. Mrs. Lincoln at the library, and apparently Tad Collins owned one. It was hanging in his bedroom."

"So what about Mr. Bellows?" Dominic asked.

"I don't know," I admitted. "According to Raven's research, he never even visited the exhibit."

Daisy sent me a text message to tell me that in his police training, Ryan had heard about some evidence in Mr. Bellows's murder. A thin piece of string had been found at the scene of the crime, but the police had no other leads.

"Jessica Walsh," a voice said. "Hand me your phone."

It was Mr. Martin. "But it's snack period," I protested. Nightshade High had a strict no-cell-phone policy except during snack period or lunch.

He held out his hand. "Hand it over."

There was no sense arguing with him. I'd be able to pick up my phone in the office after school. Still, something made me delete Daisy's text before I gave the phone to him.

"What was that all about?" Dominic asked.

"I don't know," I said. "He's new, so maybe he didn't realize I wasn't breaking the rules."

Dominic pointed to a group of girls over by the vending machines. They were all texting madly. "Maybe, but he didn't take their phones away."

"Can I borrow your phone?" I asked. "I'm going to warn Daisy."

Dominic handed over his phone. "Warn her about what?"

"Keep an eye out for Mr. Martin," I told him. "I don't want him to take your phone too."

I held the phone discreetly in my lap and texted her a message: *Our art teacher makes marionettes. Any idea what kind of string they found? If you hear anything, call me at home after school.*

Eva was obviously a fan of this guy, but I wasn't.

I got my phone back after school and checked it thoroughly. It looked like someone might have been scrolling through my text messages, which freaked me out. Not that there was anything exciting to read, but I liked my privacy. It wasn't like I'd texted *Hey, I'm a virago*, but it still bothered me. Mr. Martin had been snooping, I was sure of it, and I wanted to know why.

The next day, my phone rang and my brother's number came up. "Any news?" I asked.

"Samantha woke up!" Sean said.

"We'll be right over," I replied. I hung up and called Daisy right away.

When we got to the hospital, Samantha was sitting up. She had a haunted look in her eyes but a little bit of color in her cheeks. My brother held her hand in a death grip, but he couldn't stop smiling.

"You scared the heck out of us," Daisy scolded, after she gave her best friend a long hug.

I leaned in for a hug of my own. "I'm glad you're back in the real world."

"The doctor was here a few minutes ago and said she's made a full recovery," Sean said.

"I'm going to let Ryan know," Daisy said. "He was really worried about you, too." She stepped out of the room to make the call.

"So what happened, anyway?" I asked.

"It was the freakiest thing," Samantha said. "I was in my dorm room alone, sleeping, and then I felt like someone was in the room with me."

"And then what happened? Did you see a horse?"

"A horse?" she asked. "No, no horse. I tried to get out of bed to see who was there and I couldn't move. I was frozen and I felt like all the oxygen was being sucked out of the room. Then I guess I lost consciousness. It's been one long bad dream the whole time. I'm so glad I'm finally awake." She looked at my brother with tears in her eyes.

Ryan arrived with a bouquet of flowers. "I heard you were awake," he said, beaming at Samantha.

Soon after, her room was flooded with visitors. Word got around fast in Nightshade.

My parents arrived with Sydney and Sarah. "Samantha, when will you be released?" Mom asked. "I want you to come home with us. You can stay in Jessica's room."

"Tomorrow, I think," she replied. "And thank you, but I don't want to be any trouble."

"You could stay with us if you'd rather," Daisy said. "It's not a good idea for you to be alone in the dorms. And my house is a bit quieter than the Walsh household. That way you'll be right next door and Jessica and Sean can check on you whenever they want."

"Jessica, speaking of quiet, Poppy's with your other sisters in the waiting room," Mom said. "Why don't you go make sure the little ones are behaving?"

My sisters were absorbed with coloring books when I found them. Poppy was sprawled next to Katie, with crayons in her hand.

"Poppy, Mom thought you might want to visit Sam," I said. "I've got the rugrats for a few minutes."

"I'd love to," Poppy said. "Thanks."

I took her place next to Katie. "Has the princess come back yet?"

Katie didn't look up from her coloring book. "No, and you said you'd help find her."

My sister was mad at me and I couldn't blame her.

"I'm sorry. I've been distracted," I said. "When we get home, I'll help look for Princess Antonia."

Katie finally gave me a smile. "You promise?"

"Promise," I said.

Poppy came back about half an hour later. "Your

mom asked me to take you guys home," she said. "I guess they'll be here a while longer. They want to talk to the doctor, since Sam's mom isn't here. I'm taking your parents' van and they're riding back with Sean."

We herded my sisters into our family van.

"Want me to come in?" Poppy offered when we got home.

I shook my head. "That's okay. I can handle them for a few hours."

Katie and I searched the house top to bottom for the mischievous doll. Finally, I collapsed on the couch, exhausted. Katie tried to coax me to get up and search some more.

"We've looked all over, Katie."

"Not at Natalie's," she said. "We should look there." The dollhouse had come from Natalie and Slim's attic, so she had a point.

Plus, Natalie might be able to help me with Selena's black magic lead. She didn't practice black magic, but her grandmother had when she was alive.

"I'll go over there tonight," I said.

"I want to go with you," Katie said. "Princess Antonia might be there. She was looking for a present for the prince."

"We'll go as soon as Mom and Dad get home," I assured her.

It was dark before they walked through the door, which meant there was no way Mom was going to let us ride our bikes.

"Could you please give us a ride?" I begged.

"Why do you want to go to Slim and Natalie's anyway?" Mom asked.

"Princess Antonia is there," Katie said.

"How did your doll end up at Natalie's?"

"She walked there," Katie replied.

Mom thought she was being sassy and frowned. She didn't know the doll could move on her own. Then she gave me an exasperated look, but after a few seconds nodded. "Ask your dad to drive you," she said. "But don't bother Natalie and Slim if they're busy."

Dad drove us to the house and waited in the car while we rang the doorbell.

Natalie answered. "Jessica, Katie, come in," she invited. She was a short, curvy young woman with blond hair. Her horn-rimmed glasses were askew.

"Hi, Natalie," I said. "I don't want to bother you, but I need some information about witchcraft."

"Of course," she replied. "I was just working on this tricky spell."

Katie amused herself by searching for the princess while Natalie and I sat on the couch and talked.

"Selena Silvertongue mentioned there could be a black

magic link to the recent murders," I explained. "Could someone really try to murder someone using a painting? If they used black magic?"

"It's possible," she said. "But they'd have to get something belonging to the victim and put it into the painting somehow."

"Like painting it in there?"

"No," she said. "Like burning the item in a ritual and then mixing the ash into the paint. Or even keeping the item and using it in a spell."

"It seems like a lot of work," I commented. "Jensen Kenton is the obvious suspect, but I can't figure out a motive."

"Some people are just evil, Jessica," Natalie replied. "If there's hate in their heart, using black magic will only make it worse."

"Thanks, Natalie," I said. "You've been a huge help."

"Katie, we'd better go," I told my sister. I didn't expect the tears.

"But I haven't found the princess," she said. "Can I look in the attic?"

"Is it okay, Natalie? She's really worried about her."

"It's fine, but why would she go up there?" Natalie asked.

"Good question. Katie, did she say what she wanted?"

Katie shook her head. "Just a present."

As we went up the stairs, we heard an angry hissing noise coming from a corner of the attic.

"That's not good," Natalie said. "It sounds like Tigger caught something." She broke into a run.

Natalie's tabby had the princess cornered. The cat's claws were extended and his ears were back as he snarled at the doll, who rode a tiny black horse. Princess Antonia's cornflower blue gown was shredded.

"Shoo, kitty!" Katie said.

Natalie scooped up her cat, ignoring his attempts to wiggle out of her grasp. "I'll put him in my bedroom," she said.

Katie stooped down to examine her doll. "She's hurt!"

"Natalie can fix her," I soothed.

Natalie came back and took a look at the princess. "She's bleeding."

The princess stomped her tiny feet. "Do not touch me, witch!"

I leaned down and looked her in the eyes. "Mind your manners, princess."

The little doll smiled sweetly. "Of course. I have found something for the prince's birthday present. His favorite steed."

"Great," I said. "Now we're going home."

I scooped her and the minihorse into the Tupperware container I'd brought. I didn't put the lid on it, but it was too deep for her to climb out of.

"Thanks, Natalie," I said. "I hope she learned her lesson, but call me if you see her around again."

On the way home, I had to turn up the radio in Dad's car so he wouldn't hear the princess's tiny shrieks of rage.

CHAPTER **SIXTEEN**

My whole family had tickets to the circus on Saturday night. Mom had even bought one for Dominic.

He pulled up at dusk, just as I was trying to help my dad get my sisters into the van.

"Ready to go?" he asked.

"I'm riding with Dominic," I said quickly.

"Can I come with you?" Katie asked.

"If it's okay with Dominic," Mom said.

I looked at my boyfriend, who grinned. "C'mon, Katie, let's get your seat into my car."

Since she was seven years old, Katie hated it when we called it a car seat, even though it was one.

It was definitely an old-fashioned circus. We sat on hay bales, but Dominic had very considerately brought a couple of blankets, which he spread out on the bales for us.

"How did you know?" I asked.

"I've been to the circus before," he said. "This one is an equestrian show."

"Which means?"

"Which means that they'll have horses. Lots of them."

The ringmaster strode into the arena. She was tall and curvaceous and wore a red and gold lame suit and a tiny black top hat. Every guy in the audience leaned forward at the sight of her.

Six pure white horses pranced in. Unlike the one we'd seen on the beach, they didn't have red eyes. There were three acrobatic clowns riding on their backs.

This would be a perfect place for a Mara to hide. I glanced around the audience. I was sure Sanja wouldn't be able to resist a circus, and I spotted her in a corner. Her eyes were glued on the horses.

I turned my attention back to the performance. Something about one of the clowns looked familiar.

Katie sat next to me. Her fact was rapt as she stared at the prancing animals.

I leaned in and whispered to Dominic, "That's Tashya, isn't it?"

There was a long pause. "Yes, but please don't say anything at school. She'd kill me."

"I won't," I said. "Unless I find out that she was involved in the murders somehow."

"Tashya would never kill anyone," he said.

"I hope you're sure of that."

"I am," he said. But he didn't sound that sure.

Just then, my tattoo began to burn.

A ghostly white horse stomped into the ring. It let out a terrifying sound, like someone screaming in pain, and then reared up on its hind legs. Its eyes gleamed red and a thick fog rolled into the tent.

At first, everyone thought it was part of the act, but then the horse screeched again.

It nearly struck one clown on the forehead, but another clown pushed her out of the way. Then the horse kicked the poles that supported the tent, over and over. One went crashing down and narrowly missed the stands.

There was sudden chaos as the big top filled with screams. People were jumping over rows and running for the exit.

Dominic scooped Katie up in his arms and put her on his shoulders. "Hang on tight, Katie," he said. "Don't let go no matter what."

My mom and dad calmly stood up. Dad put Kellie on his shoulders and told Sarah and Sydney to hold hands with Grace and Fiona. My sisters did exactly as my parents told them, but I could tell Gracie was scared.

"This way," Dominic said. He pointed in the opposite direction from where most people were headed. "There's another exit over here."

"I have to find Sanja," I said. "You guys go ahead."

To my surprise, my parents didn't argue with me. I searched the crowd, but I didn't see her. Unless there was another Mara in town, I feared she had transformed into the out-of-control creature in the tent.

There was a toddler crying for his mother. He was headed dangerously close to the Mara. I ran over and snatched him up.

Most of the crowd had already made it outside, but I spotted a scared ten-year-old from Grace's class and grabbed her, too. I never found Sanja.

Outside, things were much calmer. There was a squad car and an emergency vehicle already on site. A few people had bumps and bruises, but it didn't look like anyone had been seriously hurt.

I found Grace's classmate's dad and then went looking for the toddler's mom. She was in tears, trying to go back into the tent. She practically strangled me with a hug when I handed over her little boy.

My family was sitting at the picnic table. Sarah was texting furiously on her phone and Sydney had found a boy from her class to flirt with.

Dominic was trying to keep Katie occupied, but I noticed she kept scanning the crowd. She broke into a huge smile when she saw me.

"Jessica, there you are!" she said. "Wasn't the circus fun?"

Leave it to my sister to think that a rampaging Mara made for great entertainment.

"Did you find Sanja?" Dominic asked.

I shook my head. "I didn't see her anywhere," I said. "But she didn't do this. I'm sure of it."

Anton Platsky overheard me. "Don't be too sure of that," he said. "You don't know what my daughter is capable of." Then he walked away.

I stared after him. If his daughter was a Mara, could he be one too?

"Let's go home, gang," Dad said. "I've had about as much circus as I can take."

CHAPTER SEVENTEEN

I tried to take my mind off the circus disaster by staying up late doing homework on Saturday night. It was hard keeping my grades up with all the stuff that was happening in Nightshade.

I must have dozed off, because my head was on my desk when a thumping sound woke me. The lights flickered and went out. I reached under my bed and grabbed one of the flashlights Mom had bought us right after our big disaster preparedness assembly at school.

I listened, but there didn't seem to be anyone else awake in my house. Everything was quiet, but my tattoo tingled.

I tiptoed downstairs and stood on the bottom step listening. The sound that had woken me up didn't come again, but something made me cross to the living room window and peer outside.

Standing near the streetlight was the same clown I'd seen at Eva's. The clown's mouth was dripping blood and its eyes glowed red. My chest went tight and my heart felt like it had dropped to my toes. The clown saw me and laughed. The long screechy sound was familiar, like I'd heard it many times before, but I couldn't place where.

Was I dreaming? If so, I was going to take control. I slipped out the back door, determined to catch the maniacal clown by surprise.

The grass was wet with dew and cold on my bare feet as I walked through the side yard to the front of our house. I kept to the shadows so the clown wouldn't see me. I was about fifty feet away when the clown realized I was there and started to run.

I followed. Dream or reality, I wasn't going to let this creep intimidate me.

Virago training was paying off. I had almost caught up to the clown. When I was about a foot away, I reached out and caught hold of its oversize polka-dot shirt. I tugged hard and the fabric ripped. Off-balance, I fell backwards and hit my head on the hard pavement, and then everything went black.

There was a persistent ringing in my ears. It hurt to open my eyes, but I did it anyway. I was lying in my own bed and my alarm was blaring. I leaned over and slammed the off button.

It had been just a dream. Or had it? I touched the

back of my head. It was sore and there was a lump where I'd hit the pavement. I got out of bed and looked for clues. My room was just as I'd left it the night before, but grass clung to my pajama bottoms.

So it *hadn't* been a dream. Which meant there was a real clown stalking me. How had I gotten back into my room? I searched my memory, but it was blank.

"Jessica, come down here, please," Mom hollered. She did not sound pleased.

"On my way," I replied. I put on jeans and my favorite Side Effects May Vary tee and went downstairs.

"Can you explain this?" she asked. She pointed to muddy footprints all over the front hallway.

"No, I can't." It was the truth. I couldn't explain it, not without complicating my life. Besides, Mom probably wouldn't have believed me anyway.

She gave me a long-suffering sigh. "Could you please clean it up?"

"I'll get right on it," I said. But first, I was going to grab my cell phone and snap a photo to show Flo.

I took photos of the footprints from several different angles and then got out the mop and cleanser. While I was cleaning, I noticed a scrap of fabric clinging to the throw rug.

"Jessica, are you almost finished?" Mom asked. "Mrs.

Devereaux is meeting me here today. I'm going to show her a couple of places."

"Sam's mom is moving back to Nightshade?" I asked. I stuffed the fabric into my pocket when she wasn't looking.

"She's thinking about it. She wants Samantha to move out of the dorms and move in with her."

Sam didn't get along with her mom very well and I didn't really blame her. Her mom had basically abandoned her when she took off for San Francisco years ago.

"Is Sam going with you?"

"No," Mom replied. "She's still not feeling up to it."

"Is she still staying at the Giordanos'?" I asked. "Maybe I'll go over and see how she's feeling."

"That's very kind of you," Mom said.

"Don't sound so surprised," I said.

"That's not what I meant. It's just I didn't get the impression that you cared for Samantha all that much."

"She's growing on me," I admitted. "There's more to Sam than I once thought."

I rounded up Katie, who was in her room playing with her dollhouse.

"The prince and princess don't want to play," she said sadly.

"Why not?"

"They just want to make googly eyes at each other," Katie said. "Like you and Dominic."

I laughed. "They're in love."

"Are you and Dominic in love?" Her blue eyes were filled with curiosity. I squirmed and quickly changed the subject.

"I have something that will cheer you up," I said.

"I doubt it," she sniffed.

"We're going to visit Daisy and Samantha."

"Why didn't you say so?" She jumped up and tore down the stairs so fast that I barely had time to grab my phone.

Rose answered the bell. "Daisy and Samantha are in the back," she said.

The two of them were sitting at the patio table. There was a plate of fruit and a pitcher of orange juice on the table, but Sam's plate looked untouched.

"Jessica, come join us," Daisy said. "Have a glass of juice. Sam hasn't eaten anything." She sounded worried.

Katie practically knocked me over to sit next to Sam. When I saw that it made Samantha smile, I didn't even mind.

"So did you find out anything new?" Daisy asked me in a low voice.

I glanced at my sister. Katie was telling Samantha some story about her classroom, so their attention wasn't on us.

"Something weird happened last night," I said. I described the clown's late-night visit and then said, "I don't think I was dreaming. I have the lump on my head to prove it."

"It sounds like it was someone who just wanted to scare you," she said. "Otherwise, you probably would not have ended up in your room."

"Flo will make me go get checked out at the doctor," I said glumly. "And then I'll have to make up something to tell my mom."

"Don't tell her, then," Daisy suggested.

"Yeah, right."

"I've got some cinnamon rolls baking. I think they're ready. Do you girls want some?" Daisy asked.

"I'm not very hungry," Samantha said.

"Are you okay?" I asked. "How are you sleeping?"

She shrugged. "Not so great."

Daisy went to the kitchen and came back with fat, delicious cinnamon rolls still steaming from the oven and glasses of milk.

Even Sam couldn't resist, and we dug in.

"Daisy, you are such a great cook," I said.

When her plate was clean, Sam said, "I did remember something that might be helpful."

"What's that?" Daisy asked.

"It was a man's voice I heard in my dreams."

"Sam, did you buy any of Jensen Kenton's paintings?" I asked.

She shook her head. "No, but my roommate did. She liked it because it reminded her of that famous painting. You know the one. I think it's called *The Scream*. The funny thing is the man in the dream kept saying my roommate's name over and over. Stacy, Stacy, Stacy," Sam said, her voice rising higher and higher with each repetition.

"We need to see that painting," I said.

Daisy grabbed her keys and drove us to UC Nightshade.

When we got to Sam's dorm room, the painting was gone.

"Stacy, what happened to that painting?" Sam asked.

Her roommate looked up from her fashion magazine. "I had a party the other night. Some jerk put his foot through it. It was destroyed."

After we grilled Stacy a little more, she revealed that the painting had been destroyed a few minutes before Sam had woken up from her coma.

"That's no coincidence," Daisy said. "That's a bona fide clue."

CHAPTER EIGHTEEN

A week later, Daisy and I had been through it over and over, but we weren't making much progress. I couldn't figure out why either Mr. Martin or Jensen Kenton would want to commit murder, and it was almost impossible to gather evidence when a murder was committed by magical means.

One afternoon, Daisy stopped by and asked, "Feel like going for a drive? On the way to my pastry lesson at the Wilders', I noticed something I wanted to show you."

"Let me check with my mom," I said. I found her in her office. "Mom, is it okay if I go for a drive with Daisy? We'll be back by dinner."

"Fine," she said absent-mindedly. "Will you be back by dinner?"

I rolled my eyes. I figured I'd better leave a note, too, and hastily scribbled one. "Yes," I said. I ran out and hopped into Daisy's car.

"I've been thinking about the case," Daisy said as she

pulled out of her driveway. "I still don't get why or how the murderer is choosing the victims. Do they have anything in common?"

"Raven asked Ms. Johns for a list of all the paintings that were sold," I said. "Tad Collins bought one. So did Marlon Sanguine. And Sam's roommate, of course. But Mrs. Lincoln, who was the first victim, didn't buy a painting. Neither did Mr. Bellows."

"Maybe they weren't killed by black magic," Daisy suggested.

"So who killed them?"

Daisy sighed. "I have no idea."

"I still think it's related to the art exhibit somehow," I said. "That could mean Javier Martin is behind it."

"Or Jensen Kenton," she replied.

"How are we going to prove someone is able to perform black magic and kill people in their sleep?" Daisy asked. "I've never heard of death by painting."

"Natalie said it can be done," I replied. "After we found out about Stacy's painting and Sam's miraculous recovery, I called her to find out if she knew of a way to break a black magic spell."

"What did she say?"

"A counterspell, which takes an experienced witch. Or you can destroy the object used in the spell. Natalie said that we needed to be certain who was behind the spell or we could do more harm than good."

"I guess we can't just trash all the art in Nightshade," Daisy said.

"Not without some kind of proof."

When we reached Phantasm Farms, I noticed something was off. There were no horses in the pasture.

A FOR SALE sign was up.

"That's what I wanted you to see," Daisy said.

"Where is everyone?" I asked.

"Maybe we should check out the old abandoned house," she suggested. "Didn't you say that's where Sanja stayed before?"

"Her dad was furious about the circus fiasco," I said.

We searched all of Phantasm Farms, but the Platskys were gone. Anton Platsky had taken Sanja and fled. There wasn't even a clue about where they had gone.

"He still thinks she is responsible for the murders," I said. "But I know Sanja wasn't a killer."

"Are you sure?"

I nodded. "Positive. You should have seen her, Daisy. She was too scared to leave that room. She may have given people nightmares, but she didn't want to hurt anyone. It wasn't her."

But it was too late to prove it, because she and her dad were on the run. And I was pretty sure it wasn't the first time.

"I wish they would have let me help them," I said.

I tried to tell myself that Mr. Platsky was just trying to protect his daughter, but I couldn't shake the memory of her lonely face staring out the window.

"What are we supposed to do now?" I asked. I wanted to throw something.

Even Daisy was stumped. "We follow the lead we have," she finally said.

"Can you see if you pick up anything from a painting?" I asked her.

"I'll try," she said. "But I have to warn you, I'm not a superpsychic. My powers are still wonky sometimes."

We spent the drive home trying to figure out a list of suspects. I added the name Tashya Bennington to the list, but erased it at the last minute.

She was a mean girl, all right, but I had decided she wasn't a killer.

Again it came down to Jensen Kenton and Javier Martin. But which one was behind the murders?

Suddenly, something occurred to me. "What if we're not dealing with just one murderer?"

Daisy nodded slowly. "At least two."

"That seems excessive, even for Nightshade," I said.

"It's the best theory we've come up with so far," said Daisy.

"I've got to get to virago training," I said. "Flo's been slacking off, but Dominic's mom has been taking over. She doesn't care if we have one murder to solve or a hundred. She puts us through our paces. Today, it's an obstacle course."

When I got to the park, Mrs. Gray stood there barking orders at Raven and Andy.

"You're late," she snapped when I jogged up. She had been nice enough last time I'd seen her, but maybe that was only for Dominic's benefit.

"Daisy and I were working on the case," I snapped back. I was sick of playing nice with her, even if she was Dominic's mom. She was never going to approve of me, at least not as long as I was dating her son and was a virago. "And besides, you're not my trainer. Flo is."

"Jessica, I want to talk to you. Now," Flo ordered. I followed her until we were out of earshot of the other viragoes.

I thought I was in big trouble, but Flo didn't read me the riot act. "I've been putting off telling you this, but Lydia is taking over as your trainer."

"What?" The dread I felt must have shown in my face, because Flo put a hand on my shoulder.

"Don't worry," she said. "It's only temporary. I'm going on tour with the band."

"On tour?" I stared at her like she was speaking a foreign language.

"With my husband," she said with a defensive edge to her voice. "I'm a newlywed, remember? I thought you, of all people, would understand."

"I d-do," I stuttered. "You just surprised me, that's all. I'm happy for you, Flo."

She finally cracked a smile. "Thanks, Jessica," she said. "Don't tell the other girls. I want to tell them myself."

We rejoined the others. Raven gave me a sympathetic look and Andy nudged me with her shoulder. They obviously thought I'd been chewed out royally.

"Laps," Mrs. Gray ordered. "Then we'll see what you're made of."

I fell into place next to Raven. "Is it hard on you?" I asked. "When your mom leaves, I mean?"

"Not like it is with Dominic," she said. "I'm a virago too, so I understand, at least a little. He resents her."

"If you're talking, you're not running fast enough," Mrs. Gray barked.

Raven and I exchanged a glance and upped our pace.

By the time practice was over, we were all groaning and sore, but I was proud of myself for keeping up with Lydia Gray. She might not ever like me, but she might learn to respect me. If I didn't die from her grueling training sessions first.

CHAPTER NINETEEN

At the Day of the Dead party, Side Effects May Vary (and maybe the free food) had brought in a full house. The Wilder estate was overrun with Nightshade residents enjoying the festivities.

"How's the ankle?" Dominic asked as we walked into the party.

"It's completely healed," I said. "Just in time to chase down bad guys. Or girls, as the case may be."

Mrs. Wilder greeted guests near the French doors which led to the garden. Elise Wilder, her granddaughter, and Bane Paxton, Elise's boyfriend, stood at her side. They were all dressed to the nines.

"Elise, I can't seem to find my lace handkerchief," Mrs. Wilder said. "The one my sister Lily made for me."

"I'll look for it, Grandmother," Elise replied.

I hadn't had to fret about what to wear, because Ms. Clare had mandated white tops and black pants or skirts for chorus members. Still, I had found a really cute pair of heels to go with the outfit and threw on a red cardi, which I'd have to take off before our performance.

The garden had been strung with lights and decorated with orange and black streamers. A booth for face painting had been set up near the hedge maze, and my sisters were all in line, even Sarah.

Katie spotted me and came running up. "Do you like my Day of the Dead face paint?" Half of her face was painted as a sugar skull, and vines and roses trailed down the other half.

"Love it!" I told her.

"Do you want to get your face painted too?" she asked. "Mr. Martin, the art teacher, is working in the booth."

Great. And I could see Jensen Kenton through the French doors, schmoozing with Mrs. Wilder. My top two suspects were at a house full of potential murder victims.

"Maybe later," I said. "I still have to sing, remember? Let's get a cookie instead. Daisy made them."

The buffet had been set up in the grand ballroom. Nightshade High's art class had arranged their marionettes in a row along one wall.

Katie scampered over to the buffet and snagged a cookie. I followed her and did the same. Circe Silvertongue, sorceress and star of her own now-canceled cooking show, got in line behind us and heard me. "Daisy made these?" She reached for a cookie and took one bite. She chewed slowly and deliberately. "Not bad," she said.

Daisy approached the buffet. "That's a high compliment coming from you," she said to the celebrity chef.

Ms. Clare was giving me a *get over here* look. The rest of the choir had already arrived, and they were obviously waiting on me.

"I'd better go," I told Daisy.

We were performing outside, where a temporary stage had been erected near the hedge maze. "Are you ready for our duet?" Dominic asked as we walked to our places.

"Ready as I'll ever be," I said.

The entire chorus sang a mash-up of Halloween favorites, and then it was time for the duet. Dominic took my hand as we stepped up to the microphone. To my relief, he stuck to the words of "Sally's Song." I was used to his breaking into random songs, but I didn't think Ms. Clare would appreciate it.

There was a generous amount of applause after our songs, but Ms. Clare didn't look happy. She was a perfectionist, so I wasn't surprised when she made us gather around for a post-performance critique.

"Harmony, you were a little pitchy," she said. "Again."

"Sorry, Mom," Harmony said. I was glad to see the criticism didn't seem to faze her, though. She'd come dangerously close to dying the last time she'd tried to become the perfect singer.

"And Connor, you came in late during the first song," she said.

I clung to Dominic's hand, certain that I was next in line for Ms. Clare's scolding. Instead, she actually cracked a smile and said, "Now go enjoy the party."

Dominic gave me a kiss. "I've got to meet the rest of the band before we go on. See you in a bit."

After he left, I found Raven. "Want to get something to eat?"

We got some cupcakes. "So did Dominic tell you about his latest prediction?" she asked.

I stopped mid-bite and stared at her. "No, he didn't. What song did he sing?"

"'Tears of a Clown,'" she said. "I was sure it was a clue. He acted all weird about it."

Suddenly, it all made sense to me. There was no sign of Tashya, but there was a familiar clown making balloons into animal shapes. I noticed her eyes following me.

She had a tiny grin at the edge of her painted mouth. Her hands twisted and twisted and something bright gleamed on her finger. It was a ring. The one Tashya had lied about when she said Dominic gave it to her.

"I'm going to kick that clown's butt," I muttered.

"Just one problem, Jess," Raven whispered. "Aren't you afraid of clowns?"

"Not when it's Dominic's ex masquerading as one to cause problems," I replied.

"Tashya? No way," she said.

I marched over to Tashya the clown. "I know it was you," I said. "Stop trying to freak me out. Dominic isn't going to break up with me."

The clown smirked at me. "I wouldn't be so sure of that."

"You're pathetic," I said. "You're gorgeous and smart and obviously a really good acrobat, and instead of being proud of who you are, you just use those talents to hurt other people."

"Nobody likes clowns," she said. "Especially you."

"Maybe I wouldn't be so scared if you hadn't been terrorizing me."

She snorted. "Terrorizing? I didn't even touch you."

"But you did," I said. "You carried me back to my room when I hit my head. What I don't understand is why."

"I don't like you," she said. "That doesn't mean I wanted to kill you or anything."

"Thank you for that," I snorted.

"I'm over it anyway," she said. "I won't bother you

again. My parents are picking me up tomorrow, so I guess this is goodbye."

"I guess it is." I wouldn't be sorry to see the last of her.

I wasn't sure Tashya was telling the truth, but it was as close to an apology as I would get. And besides, I had a few other things to worry about, like catching the real killers.

I caught up with Dominic before he went onstage and told him what had happened with Tashya.

"Wow," he said. "I never thought she'd go that far."

I shrugged. "Love makes people do crazy things, I guess," I said. "Are you sure you aren't going to break up with me?"

He wrapped his arms around me. "I'm sure." His lips touched mine briefly and then he pulled away to stare into my eyes. "Are we okay?"

I gave him another kiss. "We're more than okay."

CHAPTER TWENTY

After it got dark, the music started up and we went back to the grand ballroom for dancing. Side Effects May Vary was playing a set there. The tables were decorated with pumpkins carved into skeletal Day of the Dead faces. Lights danced on the black-and-white marble floor.

Tashya and Harmony made a beeline for a table near the band. Raven and I snagged a table across from them, and Eva and Evan wandered in and joined us. I looked around but I didn't see Flo anywhere, which was unusual. She never missed one of her husband's performances.

Side Effects May Vary took the stage. Dominic had changed out of his chorus-mandated black and white. His well-worn jeans and faded T-shirt didn't detract from his good looks, and several girls in the audience eyed him like he was as delectable as Daisy's cookies.

"This is a new song I wrote for my girlfriend, Jessica,"

he said. He started to sing, but a horrified look came over his face as Alice Cooper's "Welcome to My Nightmare" came out of his mouth instead.

One of the groupie types sitting near me started to laugh, and the sound soon echoed around the room. But I knew Dominic wasn't trying to insult me. It was a clue.

Dominic's voice trailed off. "Let's try that again," he said sheepishly. He gave me an apologetic look, but I just smiled at him.

Out of the corner of my eye, I noticed Jensen Kenton at the buffet table, his plate piled high with treats. That was when I realized that the song was a warning about him.

It dawned on me that there'd been a clue in the trunk of Mr. Kenton's car. Natalie had said the killer would need personal items from the victims to perform black magic. What I thought had been a lost-and-found box had been items Mr. Kenton had stolen in order to weave his spell.

I rushed away to search for Daisy, and found her sitting next to Ryan at a table with her sisters and their boyfriends. I sat and explained to them what I'd seen.

"We have to capture him," Daisy said. "And then we have to destroy those paintings."

"I'm on it, but it sounds like something I need to run

by the Nightshade City Council," Ryan said. "Nicholas, do you know where your dad is?"

"He was standing by the desserts the last time I saw him," Nicholas said. "I'll go with you. We can at least ask Mr. Kenton some questions, right?"

Ryan nodded. "Let's go."

After they left, Daisy explained. "Mr. Bone and the city council are in charge of regulating paranormal activities for Nightshade. But don't worry, Ryan will get the okay to destroy every painting."

Sean and Samantha joined us. "I thought you guys weren't going to make it," I said.

"I know," Sean said. "But Sam is feeling a lot better and she wanted to see everyone."

It made me a little nervous that my entire family was here. "We survived Sean's Grad Night," I muttered. "We can survive this."

A shadow crossed Samantha's face. Why had I mentioned Grad Night? Her father killed someone that night.

"I'm sorry, Sam," I said. "I didn't mean to . . ." But she was already gone.

Daisy's phone jingled and she checked it. "That's not good," she said. "Ryan just sent me a text. Mr. Kenton has vanished. They're heading to the art exhibit now to look for him and to — take care of the paintings."

Flo finally came in and ambled over to where we were sitting. She had dressed for the occasion with a brand new T-shirt that said BOO! and a pair of jeans.

The band started up again, but then Jeff Cool stomped off in the middle of the set.

"What's wrong now?"

Raven came over. "Dom started to sing an Iggy Pop song and Jeff lost it."

"What song?" Andy asked.

"'Little Doll,'" Raven said. "By the Stooges."

"It's a clue," I told Flo in a whisper. "A doll."

"Do you think it has something to do with Katie's dollhouse?" she asked.

"No, not that. The marionettes. Mr. Martin," I said. We both turned toward the art teacher, who was standing across the room with a marionette dancing in his hands, its eyes sparkling.

"Ugh," Raven said. "Puppets."

"They found a string like the ones Mr. Martin uses at the scene of the shop teacher's murder," I said. "Puppet string." Mr. Martin saw our suspicious expressions and threw the marionette he'd been holding, then bolted for the door.

Poppy and her boyfriend, Liam, were holding hands, but she dropped Liam's hand and rushed over to us. "What was that?"

"Stop him!" I shouted. Flo ran to overtake Mr. Martin and took a swing at him, but he ducked. He sidestepped her and made a run for the door, but didn't get far before one of Andy's martial arts stars whizzed by his head. Clamping an arm around Flo's neck, Mr. Martin dragged her with him.

An angry mob of my friends and family was behind him.

Poppy's psychic power was telekinesis. "Is there any way you can stop him?" I yelled to her.

She nodded. A few seconds later, a marionette flew into the air and hit Mr. Martin. He let go of Flo and kept running.

Flo was madder than ever. She picked up Eva's Vincent Price puppet and hurled it at Mr. Martin's head. He went down with the blow, then scrambled up again, but Dominic put out a long, gorgeous leg and tripped him. Mr. Martin went sprawling, and Dominic grabbed him by his collar and hauled him to his feet.

Raven snatched up the other marionettes and moved them out of reach. Daisy yanked some of the string off the marionettes and used it to tie up Mr. Martin. As soon as he was out of commission, I went looking for Chief Wells. I didn't want to take any chances.

"Where's the chief?" I asked Bianca, the Wilder's Restaurant hostess.

"I already called her," Bianca said. "She was outside in her patrol car."

As soon as Lola Wells arrived, she cuffed Mr. Martin and read him his rights.

I was glad Daisy and the other viragoes had been around to help me. Maybe I'd been wrong and Mr. Martin, not Jensen Kenton, was responsible for all the murders.

An hour later, the festivities seemed to be back on track. Connor's band, Magic and Moonlight, was playing a set, and Dominic pulled me onto the dance floor during a slow song. I put my head on his shoulder and relaxed.

A few songs later, there was a tap on my shoulder.

"Have you seen my grandmother?" Elise Wilder asked.

"She was talking to Jensen Kenton earlier," I said. "But I haven't seen her lately."

Elise's eyes glowed red and I took a step back. "I think there's something wrong."

"I'll help you look for her," I volunteered.

CHAPTER TWENTY-ONE

We searched the mansion, but didn't find Mrs. Wilder.

"Has anything unusual been happening to your grandmother lately?" I asked when I saw how agitated Elise was.

"She's been having bad dreams," she said simply.

"She didn't happen to buy a painting from Jenson Kenton, did she?"

"She didn't buy one," Elise said slowly. "But he gave her one. It's hanging in the restaurant. She took it because she didn't want to hurt his feelings, but Grandmother said she didn't want it in the private areas of the house. It gave her the creeps."

We raced to the restaurant, where the painting was hanging next to the front desk. It depicted a werewolf drowning in liquid silver. I looked around for something to destroy it with, and, after several crucial seconds ticked by, found a letter opener and slit the canvas apart. Then

I yanked the frame off the wall and stomped the painting into pieces.

There was no silver anywhere at the Wilder estate. Silver. Werewolves. I was beginning to understand the problem.

"I hope it worked," Elise said. Then she raised her head and sniffed the air. "I smell blood," she said. She ran faster than I'd ever seen a girl in heels run.

I jogged after her and caught up to her in an isolated area of the garden. Her grandmother sat in a white wicker chair. At first it looked like she'd simply fallen asleep, but Mrs. Wilder was dead. A thin line of blood trickled from her mouth. A cup of tea had spilled onto the ground and had stained the earth.

Elise started to howl. It was a long, mournful cry that seconds later echoed throughout the estate.

One by one, they came. Elise's boyfriend, Bane Paxton, came first and took her into his arms as she sobbed onto his shoulder.

Bane's brother, Wolfgang, was the next to arrive, and then their parents. More and more people appeared, and each took up the mournful howl. I realized I was surrounded by a werewolf pack. Ryan Mendez stepped forward and closed the circle. I saw Daisy and her sisters standing in the shadows. I wanted to join them, but I was trapped inside the ring of werewolves. I wasn't scared though.

Bianca came, but stood just outside the circle. She was silent, but her fingers had lengthened into claws.

The desolate cries grew louder until they welled into one unified shriek. Answering howls came from distant points all around us.

When it stopped, I stepped closer to Mrs. Wilder, and Bane let out a low growl.

"It's all right, Bane," Elise said.

I bent down to look at the teacup. I knew enough not to touch it. There was a strange powder at the bottom.

"Ground-up silver," Nicholas Bone said. I hadn't even heard him approach.

Ryan was behind him. "We got to all the paintings that were left," he told us. "But some are unaccounted for."

"Like which ones?"

Ryan cleared his throat. "One titled *Silver*."

Elise growled, her eyes glowing a fierce red. "We must find this painter Jensen Kenton."

"Elise, don't," Daisy said.

But she was already gone.

"If he's the murderer, he has something of Mrs. Wilder's on him," I said. "We need to find Jensen before Elise does."

"Let's split up," Ryan said. "Daisy and I will take the

third floor. Bane, go with Jessica and check the second floor."

"He's probably long gone," Daisy said.

"I hope for his sake he is," Bane said grimly. "Elise will rip him apart."

We found Jensen hiding in the kitchen.

"Pretty smart," Bane said. "All the food smells mask his scent."

"Pretty guilty, I'd say," I replied.

"A wolf just tried to eat me," Jensen said in a trembling voice. "Help me."

I saw a lace handkerchief sticking out of his pocket. The one that Mrs. Wilder had mentioned missing earlier.

"Why did you murder Mrs. Wilder? She was a good person."

"Good person?" he snorted. "Like that matters."

Elise reappeared in the doorway. "It matters to me," she snarled, and her jaw elongated as her teeth grew longer and sharper.

I started to lay a comforting hand on her shoulder, but Bane stopped me. "I wouldn't do that," he said. "Not now."

"You're an artist," I said to Jensen. "Why would you kill anyone?"

"I wasn't an artist," he said. "I used to be an artist. A bad one. But black magic changed all that. I found a new outlet for my . . . creative impulses."

"You're right, you're not an artist," I said. "You're just evil."

The chief of police and Deputy Denton arrived, which probably saved Jensen's life.

"We'll take it from here," Chief Wells said. "Thanks, Daisy and Jessica."

"But Chief, he killed my grandmother!" Elise said.

"All the more reason to let the law deal with him," she replied.

After a pause, Elise nodded. "Make sure the city council knows what happened."

Chief Wells read Jensen his rights and then cuffed him before the deputy led him away.

"Thank you all for your help tonight," the chief said to us. "But there are a few things I don't understand. Why would a high school art teacher kill anyone?"

"Mrs. Lincoln was his aunt," I said. "And Mr. Martin killed her for an inheritance."

"But she died with a look of horror on her face, just like the nightmare victims," Daisy said. "That confused us for a little while. Until we realized that she must have been truly aghast that her nephew was trying to kill her. Mrs. Lincoln didn't make a big deal about it, but she was worth a lot of money and Javier Martin was her only heir."

"What about Mr. Bellows, the shop teacher?" Chief Wells asked.

"Mr. Martin must have killed him, too," I said. "He used the wood shop at school to carve his diabolical puppets. Then he used the gemstones he stole from his aunt's jewelry for his marionettes. The shop teacher must have realized he was covering up his crime."

"We should be able to match the string found at the crime scene with the string Mr. Martin used for his puppets," the chief said.

"He must have been desperate for money," I said.

"Or he was just crazy," Daisy replied.

"One doesn't cancel the other out," Chief Wells said drily.

Dominic wrapped his arms around me. "Hey, I've been looking all over for you."

"Mrs. Wilder . . ." I didn't finish my sentence because I realized Bane and Elise were standing next to him.

"I heard. I'm so sorry, Elise," Dominic told her.

"I know my grandmother wasn't a young woman," she replied. "But I can't believe she's been murdered."

"I'm sorry we didn't make it in time to save her," I said.

"You tried, Jessica," she said. Mrs. Wilder had been a lovely, gracious person who was a legend in Nightshade. I wondered what would happen to Wilder's Restaurant, and, more importantly, to Elise.

Lily and Balthazar Merriweather rushed up.

"Where is she?" Lily asked. "Where is my sister?"

Daisy stepped forward. "I have some bad news. Mrs. Wilder is dead."

My head was spinning. How on earth could Mrs. Wilder and Lily Merriweather be sisters? Mrs. Wilder had been in her eighties and Lily couldn't be much older than Flo.

"Aunt Lily, I can't believe Grandmother is gone," Elise said. Lily broke into loud sobs.

Daisy took Lily by the hand. "You've had a shock, Lil," she said. "Sit down and I'll get you some water."

It took hours before everything was sorted out.

"What should we do with all the marionettes?" I asked.

"Load them up in my van," Flo said. "We'll go burn them in the dumpster outside the diner. After we remove the jewels from their eyes, of course."

"I want to keep my Vincent Price puppet," Eva protested.

"Why don't you make a new one instead?" I suggested. "I'm not sure you want something Mr. Martin helped you with."

"You're right," she said glumly. "Maybe I can make two of them this time. A young VP and an old one."

"Maybe I should just buy you the poster," Evan said.

We all laughed.

"You're right," Eva said. "After tonight, I never want to see a puppet again. Unless it's on *Sesame Street*."

"You still watch *Sesame Street*?" Andy asked.

"What? I can't watch scary stuff all the time," Eva replied. "And besides, Big Bird rocks."

She had a point.

"This place is a mess," I said. "We should clean up so Elise doesn't have that to deal with on top of everything else."

Bianca overheard me. "Go ahead and go home, Jessica," she said. "Mrs. Wilder" — she cleared her throat before she continued — "Mrs. Wilder arranged a cleaning crew. They'll be here first thing in the morning."

"Let's go to Slim's," Flo said. "I didn't have time to eat tonight."

"But it closed for the party," Ryan said.

She gave him a tiny smile. "I know the owner."

"I don't feel like being alone right now," Eva admitted. "It's been quite an eventful night."

"I know I should go home and get some sleep," I said. "But I'm too wired."

"Me, too," Daisy said.

"It's settled, then," Dominic said. "We'll meet everyone at Slim's."

Dominic and I got into his car, but he didn't start it up right away. "I was worried about you tonight," he said. "A little freaked out, even."

I inhaled. Had the evening been too much for him? "I know it's tough for you, me being a virago," I said softly. "But I can't help who I am."

"I know," he said. "My mom was wrong, you know. You're not like she is. She pushes everyone away. You don't."

"Speaking of your mom," I said. "Where was she tonight?"

"You're not going to believe it," he said, "but she's on a date."

I waited to see what else he would say, but instead, he kissed me. A long time later, he started the car and we headed to Slim's.

"What took you so long?" Eva whispered when I slid into the booth next to her at the diner.

"Nothing," I said, but my blush gave me away.

"That must have been some nothing." She giggled.

"What are you two talking about?" Evan asked.

"Nothing," Eva and I said at the same time.

"Okay," he said. "I get it. Girl stuff." He turned his attention back to the menu.

"Poor Mrs. Wilder," Andy said.

"Poor Elise," Ryan said. Daisy leaned her head on his shoulder.

"Good work, Jessica," she said. "I can't believe we caught two killers in one night."

"The clown confused me at first," I said. "She distracted me from the real killers. But she won't be bothering anyone from now on."

"Are you sure?" Dominic asked.

"She's heading home soon," I said. "That's not a problem, is it?" I was teasing him. I already knew the answer.

He kissed me. "I'm sorry my ex dressed up like a clown and terrorized you." His breath tickled my neck. "But now I know your weakness."

"I can't believe that five people died this fall," Poppy said. "Even more would have if you and Daisy hadn't stopped them."

"I had a good time working with you, Jessica," Daisy said. "We should do it again."

Ryan gave her a long kiss. "Gotta go," he said. "Mr. Bone gets cranky if I keep the council waiting."

"But it's after midnight," I said. "You can't possibly mean that they're meeting at this hour."

He winked at me and I blushed. "I can't tell you, but that doesn't mean it's not true."

Maybe I sounded a tad too concerned that he was leaving, because Dominic gave me a kiss of my own.

Ryan smiled at Daisy. "Are you coming with me?"

"You don't have to ask me twice," she said. "Jessica, the Nightshade City Council is special. Maybe one day you'll see."

I'd thought I knew a lot about Nightshade, the city I was supposed to protect, but I was realizing I'd only scratched the surface of its secrets.

Acknowledgments

Thanks to my readers, the nicest group of people ever. Also, big thanks to the Houston Teen Book Con, where the question "What are you afraid of?" came up during my panel. This book is the answer.

SHE LOVES ME, SHE LOVES ME NOT

Six Years Later

My boyfriend had a surprise for me, but he refused to give me any hints, even though we were in his car, headed . . . somewhere.

"Ryan, you still haven't told me where we're going," I said.

"It's a surprise," he said. "Don't be so impatient, Daisy."

"You're headed toward Main Street," I said smugly. "Are you taking me to Slim's?"

He laughed. "Always the detective, aren't you?" Ryan kept his eyes on the road, but I could tell there was mischief in them.

I gave him a triumphant smile when he parked in front of the diner, but instead of heading to Slim's, he steered me across the street, toward the police station.

Ryan kissed the palm of my hand and then held up a set of keys. "Guess what I have?"

I recognized the keys. "The big surprise is in the morgue?"

When he grinned, my heart beat a little faster.

He took my hand. "Don't you remember?" he asked softly.

"Of course I remember," I replied. "Our first kiss." Ryan and I had been friends since we were little, but things had changed the night we'd snuck into the morgue to solve a mystery.

He opened the door. "After you."

There was the same beat-up metal desk and filing cabinet, but there were daisies everywhere. Daisy chains concealed the steel drawers along one wall, daisies were scattered in a path leading to a candlelight picnic, laid out on a yellow and white gingham blanket.

"How did you manage all this?"

"Chef Pierre cooked everything," he replied. "And Sam and Sean helped me decorate."

"It's beautiful," I said. "But what's the occasion?" It wasn't my birthday or anything. "Not that I'm complaining," I added.

He took a deep breath. "I know this is an unconventional place for this." His face was serious, and for a brief second I wondered if he was going to break up with me. But Ryan and I were solid, and besides, why would he make such a big effort to dump me? He would, however, make a big production out of a proposal.

Ryan plucked a daisy from one of the vases. "She loves me, she loves me not . . ."

I finished his sentence. "She loves me."

He gave me a serious look and then took another deep breath. "The flower's never wrong. Here goes, unconventional location or not."

My hand went to the locket he'd given me for my seventeenth birthday. Was Ryan Mendez going to propose to me?

"For what?" My voice trembled as I asked the question.

"For this," he said. He took a small black box out of his pocket. "Daisy Giordano, will you marry me?"

"Yes."

He kissed me. "You haven't even seen the ring yet," he joked, but his voice was choked with emotion. "It's a sapphire, as blue as your eyes."

He slid the ring on my finger, and we both stared down at it.

"You didn't have to propose just because I'm leaving town for a few months," I teased. I was starting a six-month post-grad program in New York to hone my cooking skills.

"You mean *we* are leaving town, don't you?" he asked.

"You're coming with me?" I asked incredulously. "But what about your job?"

"I took a leave of absence," he said. "My job will be waiting for me when we get back."

"Ryan, you didn't have to do that," I said.

"I didn't want to be away from you for six months," he said. "I couldn't imagine it."

I gave him a long kiss. "You're the best boyfriend ever."

"I'm not your boyfriend," he said, deadpan.

"You're not?" Then it dawned on me, and I smiled. "Okay, you're the best fiancé ever."

"I'm all packed," he said. "And I'll be able to help out at a detective agency there."

"You know what this means?" I asked.

"What?"

"That Poppy and Rose are probably already planning the wedding for us." The last few days, my two psychic sisters had been giving me strange looks and bursting into giggles at odd times.

"I have been so worried that you'd read my mind," he said. "I wanted it to be a surprise."

"It was," I told him. "The best surprise of my life."

"And it's only the beginning," he said.

"It will be hard to say good-bye to Nightshade," I said.

"Katie Walsh will be here looking after things," Ryan replied.

"Katie? Sean's sister?" I leaned out to take a look at his face. "Little Katie from next door?"

He nodded. "She's going to do big things," he said. "And she's thirteen, not so little anymore."

"That's a relief," I said. "With Jessica and Flo traveling so much with the band, Nightshade needs someone to take care of things while we're gone."

"We'll be back," Ryan said.

"Of course we will," I replied. "No matter where we go, Nightshade will always be home."

Back in the car, I put my head on his shoulder, content. I could see my future, full of adventures, mystery, friends, and family. Most importantly, I could see Ryan and me. What else did I need?